Also by Hope Sheffield

Blood Mother

The Inflatable Man

Turnabout

Hope Sheffield

The Glass Table

This is a work of fiction. Names and characters are a product of the author's imagination, and any resemblance to actual persons, living or dead, is entirely coincidental.

To my mother and father

with love and gratitude
for a lifetime of unbreakable support

Spring

Chapter One

May 1, 1997

Ron remembered sitting with his wife Marcia right here, on the front row of the synagogue, back when she was alive. She had perched rigid, tense from planning for that great day, their daughter Lauren's Bat Mitzvah. When Ron squeezed her thigh, Marcia swatted his hand with a sharp sting of diamond rings and smoothed her skirt. Lauren, chubby and spotty and heart-achingly awkward, wriggled nervously in her pink sheath dress like a sausage sizzling in its casing. But when she sang the blessing over the Torah, even Marcia cried. Those five years had vanished, poof, like a dream. Now he was almost sixty, and Lauren was eighteen and would go to college in a few months. And Marcia had been dead for five days.

"We are so sorry for your loss, Ron. If there is anything we can do, just let us know. We are thinking of you."

Ron nodded to the parade of well-wishers brave enough to approach him before the funeral ceremony. "Thank you," he recited to the sad half-smiles of East Coast cousins and Glencoe neighbors. Towards the back, a phalanx of his grim suited law partners sat shoulder to shoulder, lending the support of the firm. Rabbi Klein, the young rabbi, appeared on the dais through a side door and perched on a high-backed chair like a judge.

Attempting to transcend himself, to reach some holy detachment from the pain, Ron swept his eyes upward, past the shiny lily-decked coffin at his feet, through the immense ark housing the Torah scrolls, and higher, to the white arched ceiling of this, his sanctuary. Closing his eyes, he tried to release his soul from his body, to float above his damaged, weeping daughter, the would-be comforters in stiff clothes and stern expressions, and his wife, front and center in her best Neiman-Marcus cocktail dress concealed inside the expensive piece of furniture which they would shortly bury in the ground. He felt Lauren's shoulder brush his arm and then yank back, and his eyes flicked straight ahead, to the golden Hebrew etched in short, punchy lines into the wall behind the ark. "Don't Steal. Don't Covet. Don't Kill."

Rabbi Klein, a small black bat, squinted and approached the podium. "We are here for a very sad occasion, to mark the passing of Marcia Block, departed too soon from the lives of her husband Ron and her daughter Lauren. May her life be for a blessing. Marcia was many things – a loving wife and mother, a junior high math teacher – for this alone, we must honor her patience and compassion…."

Relieved, the crowd chuckled. Junior high kids – who could stand them? Maybe this terrible situation was somehow bearable, even amusing? Ron wondered what the crowd's mood was. Thumbs up or thumbs down, were they with him or against him? Had they already convicted him, or were they still in a delicious pondering stage, turning their slim knowledge of the facts this way and that. He stared straight ahead at the walnut box. It should be a plain pine box, that was the Jewish rule. But Reform Jews on the North Shore didn't do that, and if he did -- that would make him look chintzy. That would make him look – guilty. As he stared, he saw the coffin fill with blood, a red river forcing through its seams, first a slick, ripe trickle, and then streams, spilling through the grain, coursing down the waxed sanctuary floor to soak Italian loafers and Gucci pumps. And the children who were here, Marcia's seventh grade students and Lauren's twelfth grade friends – they would raise their feet in the air and scream. If they knew what he felt, what he had seen in the kitchen, they would never stop screaming.

"And you, Lauren," Rabbi Klein said, peering down at her through concave lenses, "you have lost your mother too soon." Lauren's eyes filled, and she flushed with shock and embarrassment and grief. "She loved you, and you were lucky to have such a mother through your whole childhood. Cherish your memories of her, and speak of her often when you have your own children. Then she will live on, a loving source of goodness and wisdom for you and the next generation."

When she had her own children – what was he talking about, that would be never. Lauren couldn't even imagine making it through the day. Of course she would remember her mother, did he think she was an idiot? When she went to college and needed someone to call

4

because she didn't have any friends because she was too weird and sad, Lauren would remember. Every holiday, every graduation – oh my god, New Trier graduation – who was she kidding, every god damn day when she needed advice or just wanted to report on her boring life – today I studied chemistry, yes, I always have trouble with equations, and I lost my sweater, the black one that you gave me, and I ate in the cafeteria by myself, a salad, yes, I'm eating enough – she would remember her mother. Her mother wasn't perfect, but she would have listened, she would have cared.

There was one memory she wanted to bury – no, to slash from her brain and incinerate and hurl into the wind like ash. But she would never be able to forget her mother's shrieks, and the sight of her, the smeared trail, like a red snail's streaks, across shattered glass. Her mother cried out, and she gestured for Lauren to stay back, danger, glass on the floor, and then she whimpered as she realized what was happening to her, that every pump of her heart sent blood spurting from slices in her back and arms and legs. That no matter what Lauren or her father did, her life was spilling unstoppably out of her body and onto the tile. That in moments, one misstep would turn her from a miracle, a pulsing spirit, into a corpse.

"We can't always know why things happen," continued Rabbi Klein, as he pushed his glasses up on his nose. "We want a good reason. That is part of being human. But who can understand the workings of the world? There may be no answer for us. Maybe God has a plan, and we can't understand it, who knows? Sometimes things happen, and we just have to deal with them. We pray to God to give us the strength to find comfort and continue after a tragedy like this one."

But why, why, why? Lauren wanted to scream, to stand up and shout. "Look at me, here on the front row! Is this real? How could this happen?" She sat shaking in her theater seat, in a black flowered dress that her mother had once helped pick out, her dark hair swept into a leaky ponytail. She was eighteen years old, the paint barely dry on her adult face, mourning her dead mother. Next to her sat her father, stiff and serious, staring straight ahead, his glasses steamy, his fine, soft hands clutching his navy suit pants. As she shook, her shoulder tapped against him. Tap, tap, her heart beat. Tap, tap, her brain throbbed, her brain that knew things that she wouldn't dare admit. Why was her mother dead? Why in heaven, and why on earth?   Her father could have reached out to her, put his arm around her, held her still, but he didn't. He had never been that kind of father, she was not Daddy's little princess, his work and position came first. There was no one to hug her now.

Yanking her daughter Maggie's damp hand, Meredith Bennett rushed from the sweet May light of a North Shore spring into the tomb of the synagogue, white and gold and oddly windowless, despite its perch on the shore of Lake Michigan. Nabbing two seats in the last row, Meredith counted herself lucky. In front of her, columns of coiffed heads bowed dutifully over their programs.

"The Lord is my shepherd, I shall not want," the crowd mumbled cooperatively.

6

This was a popular funeral. Marcia Block had been young, just fifty-five according to the *Chicago Tribune* obituary. Her students and their parents alone took up a lot of space, Meredith noted, scanning the room for other seventh graders from Maggie's class. It was sad, all of these children who had to deal with death at such a tricky age, and of course Marcia's own daughter and husband. Some attendees must be friends of the family, though she saw fewer high school students than she might have expected, given that Lauren was a senior at New Trier. That row of suits ahead of her must be Ron Block's partners. They looked cut from black construction paper, like an unfurled line of linked paper dolls. She would recognize a group of lawyers even from the back. After all, she was one herself.

"I hope I didn't miss it." Maggie clutched anxiously at her mother.

"Of course not. You're singing at the end, and it's not that late." Meredith refrained from speaking the obvious admonishment, "but if you hadn't changed clothes so many times...." She felt Maggie settle into her seat and was glad she had zipped her lip. Mothers are powerful creatures.

Pretending to smooth her skirt, Meredith half stood, in a vain attempt to glimpse Ron and Lauren Block. She didn't know the family. She had listened while Mrs. Block described the seventh grade math program for ten minutes at the curriculum open house and spoken to her for five minutes at a parent-teacher conference, and that was it. Nor did she know the detailed circumstances of Marcia Block's death. The office buzz at the Skokie Courthouse, where Meredith was an assistant state's attorney for Cook County, was that the Glencoe police had investigated and decided it was an accident.

Although she normally spent her work day prosecuting traffic offenders, shoplifters, and petty thieves – the bread and butter of North Shore criminal lawyers and a low stakes work load that allowed her to maximize her time with her two daughters, Meredith did insert herself into the occasional death investigation. And she wanted to know more about this one. After all, Mrs. Block had been Maggie's teacher. And the circumstances of her death were, well, fishy. Somehow, Marcia Block, an energetic woman with, presumably, years of life ahead of her, had fallen through her glass kitchen table and bled to death on the kitchen floor while her husband and daughter looked on. It had to have been an accident, anything else was unimaginably horrifying. But somebody better make darn sure. Other people in this room must be thinking the same thing.

The rabbi looked up and lifted his hands. Mrs. Fester, the Wilmette Junior High music teacher, stood and walked to the front. Preteens in uncomfortable clothes emerged from rows and spilled into the aisles, like the Pied Piper's rats.

"Go on." Meredith nudged Maggie, who was picking at her cuticles.

The children, about fifty of them, assembled on the stage. Brimming with information as usual, Maggie had declined to tell her mother what they were going to sing. Meredith just prayed it wasn't, "I Had a Little Dreidel," undoubtedly the extent of Wilmette Junior High's Jewish repertoire. The kids had practiced yesterday, but that wasn't much, and Maggie was definitely nervous. And their teacher had just died, and seventh graders aren't the world's most attentive or reverent students. Which made what occurred next little short of the miracle of Chanukah.

Hands folded, heads forward, eyes shining, fifty young voices tentatively began singing. "To everything – turn, turn, turn, There is a season – turn, turn, turn, And a time to every purpose under heaven." They looked so forlorn and sounded so sweet, the girls' voices high and clear, the boys' cracking, that by the time they reached, "A time to dance, a time to mourn," the sniffing and nose-blowing in the audience were almost disruptive.

When they reached the verse, "A time to kill, and a time to heal," Meredith's brain got stuck. She wondered what that meant. Was there really a time to kill, as part of the cycle of nature? Fortunately, the children seemed more concerned about balancing on their high heels and swishing their hair out of their faces than analyzing the song's deeper implications. And, understandably, they didn't know the words very well.

As Meredith groped in her purse for a Kleenex, Maggie slipped back into her seat. "It's about life," she volunteered. "There's a time for everything, so it's all okay."

"Okay," said Meredith. "You did a good job."

The rabbi stood up and raised his arms in summoning and benediction. "Will the pall bearers please come forward."

"Wait." A decisive voice interrupted, and a man in the front row rose and approached the dais. "I would like to speak, if I might," he said to the rabbi.

"Of course." The rabbi motioned toward the podium and resumed his chair.

The man stood before the congregation. Considering his extemporaneous appearance, he was surprisingly composed, his back straight, his hands poised on the lectern. He seemed accustomed to public speaking, to making his case. Tall, dark, and carefully combed and tailored, he looked like an aged plastic doll from the Sophisticate Ken collection – white button-down shirt, bespoke suit, no Speedo. Lifting his chin, he gazed at the crowd. No one moved.

"I am Ron Block, Marcia's husband. My daughter Lauren and I would like to thank you for coming here to honor Marcia on this sad day. The children just sang that beautiful song so movingly. Marcia – Mrs. Block," he corrected, "would have been touched." He paused and stared straight ahead.

"I was struck this morning, when I came here, on this lovely spring day – finally, after so much winter weather, flowers are blooming, the trees – and you can feel the sun, warm on your face. It is the kind of day Marcia struggled through the winter to get to – but she has missed it, she is gone. 'To everything there is a season,' that's what the children sang – that's what the Bible says – but how can there be death in spring, on such a beautiful day? There is something wrong with the world when such a terrible death can occur while the earth is bursting with life."

Meredith looked over at the rabbi. She half expected him to leap up and defend God, but he sat politely. Surely he had heard this one before.

"Marcia was a wonderful woman," Ron said abruptly. Now he looked stern, as if he were lecturing the group. "She was an excellent wife and mother. Lauren and I will miss her, and we will never forget her.

We hope you will join us later at our home, where we will be sitting shiva. Thank you again for coming." Dignified despite his somewhat odd need to bare his philosophical concerns and to behave as a host at this event, Ron descended to his seat.

"Poor Lauren," said Maggie, squeezing her mother's arm. "She's Mrs. Block's daughter."

"Yes indeed," said Meredith, squeezing back.

Susie Steinmetz hated greeting the bereaved. That was the payment due for attending a funeral, which could be kind of interesting if you weren't actually sad, which she wasn't. Even though her daughter Mindy and Lauren Block were best friends all through high school, Susie didn't really know Lauren's mother Marcia. The girls were old enough to handle their own social lives. When they were freshmen and sophomores, their mothers had dropped them off at each other's front doors and waited in the car afterwards for them to pop out and hop back in. Once they could drive, even that contact disappeared. Marcia must have been at some of the picture-taking gatherings before the Turnabout and Homecoming dances, but there were always a lot of parents, and Susie just mingled with the people she knew from back when Mindy was in elementary school – nursery school, truth to tell. The Blocks had moved to Glencoe from Chicago only four years ago, so they weren't really part of the parent crowd.

The funeral had been worth it, Susie thought, shuffling down the line, closer to the inevitable awkward moment. She didn't think she had ever seen Ron Block before, she would have remembered him. He was awfully good looking, and brainy too. And there was something so touching about a man with a dead wife. And she died in such an awful way! Susie couldn't imagine how horrible it would be to find her own husband Joel bleeding profusely on the kitchen floor as he crawled toward the phone to call 911. She shook her head a little to knock the ugly picture out of it.

But you had to wonder, in this weird situation, if she fell all by herself. Ron could have killed her – maybe by accident, he just gave her a little push. Or what if he were angry about something, and in the heat of the moment, boom, crunch. Or maybe he was having an affair, he was awfully handsome, a silver fox some would say. Well, if he did kill her, that certainly complicated this whole greeting line situation. Should she express her condolences to a man who might secretly be rubbing his hands with delight? He hadn't sounded happy when he gave his speech, but he hadn't cried either. And he was a lawyer Mindy said, he could probably sound like anything at all.

Mindy nudged her shoulder. "Mom, scoot up. I've got to get to Lauren. She needs me."

A gap had opened in front of Susie, and she teetered ahead on her spring high heels. It was nice to be dressed up for a change. She and her husband Joel hadn't done anything fun lately, not since his colon cancer diagnosis back in February. No reason for her to wear pretty shoes to mop up vomit and sit in front of the TV while his hair fell out. If Mindy hadn't been so worried about Lauren, and if Susie didn't have the stress of dispensing words of comfort, this funeral would be almost a treat.

Oh god, she was on. "Lauren," she said, grabbing for the girl's closest body part, "I am so sorry for your loss." Simultaneously, Mindy let out a little cry, rushed forward, and threw her arms around her friend. Lauren buried her head on Mindy's shoulder and began to sob. Susie bit her lip and hoped that Lauren's mascara would not ruin Mindy's pale pink blouse. Clearly, Susie was not going to get much out of Lauren. As the suit ahead of her cleared, she stepped around Lauren to the main event.

Ron Block cast his eyes a considerable distance down to greet Susie, a mere five foot two soaking wet, as her mother used to say. In a plum pencil skirt and cream cashmere sweater, a pearl necklace resting demurely on her clavicle, she was glad she hadn't dressed too somberly. She was still pretty at age forty-three, and considerably younger than he was – and than Marcia had been. Just seeing her ought to cheer him up a little.

He bowed slightly. "Thank you for coming," he said. Next to him, Lauren clung to Mindy. "Your daughter?" he asked.

"Yes." Susie nodded, grateful that he had opened the conversation. "I don't know if we'll be able to pry them apart."

"That's fine," Ron said. "I'm glad Lauren has someone. She can stay with us, if it's alright with you. You could pick her up at the shiva."

"Of course," said Susie. "I am so sorry for your loss."

Ron nodded and looked toward the next person in line, a large old lady in a black suit made out of upholstery fabric. She must be an out-of-town relative, Great Aunt Sylvia from Brooklyn or something.

13

Dismissed, Susie glanced at the next receiving mourners, probably Marcia's siblings, and decided to bug out of line and be on her way. She had done her duty, she didn't need to deal with every Tom, Dick and Harry related to Marcia Block.

Exiting the synagogue lobby into the parking lot, Susie tilted her face to the May sun, a warm kiss after a tough winter. Ron was right, it was a glorious day. The sky was blue with wispy white clouds, perfect, like a cartoon. No longer gray sticks, the trees along the road were speckled with baby leaves. The day promised life and hope and joy. Maybe, for all his intellect, Ron wasn't listening to this plain message from God. Ron was alive, and so was Susie, and so were Mindy and Lauren. Joel was sick, and that was hard, but the doctor said he would get better. Marcia's death was shocking and sad, but they had marked that today, and tomorrow they could look ahead with gratitude for this beautiful world. Susie got in her car and headed toward Foodstuffs to pick up a quiche for the shiva. Today was for duty, she thought, feeling adult. But it was spring, after all. Soon everyone would be smiling again.

Chapter Two

After the funeral, Meredith decided that world happiness would increase if the Block family didn't have to listen to the babblings of another random parent in the receiving line, and if she heeded her daughter Maggie's inappropriate whine that she was dying of starvation. So she headed to the Pancake House, where, at 12:45 on Thursday afternoon, there was no line at all. Transitioning through the hallway rimmed with benches for the Sunday brunch crowd, Meredith opened the inner door to a Tiffany-lit sanctuary thick with the aroma of bacon and sautéed sugar.

"Two, please," Meredith said to a bored hostess idling near the cash register.

"Kid's menu?" The hostess, who looked barely out of junior high herself, waved a package of crayons wrapped in a griddle-themed word search in Maggie's direction.

"No thanks. Two adults."

Meredith glanced skeptically at adult number two, who was practically decking waitresses in her rush to sit, order, and receive food. Meredith tailed Maggie past the fireplace and the cocoa machine to a cozy booth at the back of the restaurant. According to the rules of the Pancake House, anyone over age ten was an adult. As Maggie knew from the insane number of Bat Mitzvahs she had attended this year, as well as from Meredith's weak attempts at religious education, she was also an adult according to Judaism. Maggie was fully responsible for her own moral behavior. Also, more important for this venue, she could eat a lot.

Maggie drummed her fingers impatiently on the wooden table. "I know what I want," she muttered.

Adults were supposed to be able to wait. "After lunch, I'll drop you back at school. You can take the bus home as usual and stay with Lucy. Let's see, it's Thursday, she has After School Sports, so she'll be a little late." Meredith opened her menu.

"I know, Mom. Just because my math teacher died doesn't mean I'm a moron." Hypoglycemia plus adolescence equals crab. "I take care of Lucy all the time."

"Not all the time," Meredith countered, taking the bait to defend her mothering commitment.

"All the time 'til you get home from work," Maggie retorted. She made work sound like a swear word.

A waitress in a white blouse, maroon skirt, and black bow tie stopped by with a pot of coffee. "What can I get you?"

"I'll have the pecan pancakes," Meredith announced recklessly. She had suffered enough today, she decided, sucking her extra five pounds under her belly button. "And coffee."

"You, Miss?" she turned to Maggie.

"Pigs-in-a-blanket, please.   And a small orange juice."   Maggie pinched her lips together primly and offered up her menu.

Meredith smiled, watching her daughter teeter toward maturity. Although Maggie would never admit it, she was looking a lot like her mother these days. They both had bunches of curly dark hair, warm brown eyes, wire-frame glasses, and a tendency to squeezable tummy and derriere. At ten, little sister Lucy was a matzo ball, but Maggie had a waist. She tugged self-consciously at the dark skirt Meredith had unearthed for this surprise somber event.

"So." Meredith stirred a minute drop of cream into her coffee. "What did you think of the funeral?"

"It was my first one.   I don't have a lot to compare it to."

"Exactly," said Meredith. "I'm not asking you if it deserved three and a half stars. What I mean is, are you okay?"

"Yeah, fine. Did we sing all right?" She sipped her orange juice, and some color returned to her face.

"It was lovely." Good, this was all about Maggie. "It seemed to mean a lot to Mr. Block."

"Yeah.   But, I mean, what was that speech anyway?"

"I'm not sure." Meredith constructed her answer as charitably as possible. "Sometimes when people are very sad, they would rather talk about something else." Also if they are not so sad, she thought.

"I get that.   Oooo, yum."   Maggie gazed appreciatively at the ramekin of pancake tubes that the waitress had placed before her and reached for her mini pitcher of syrup.

17

"Do you have any questions about – what happened to Mrs. Block?" It seemed best to confront this head-on. Who knew what frightening stories were churning through the junior high's collective brain.

"No. I don't really get it. It seems like a terrible accident. I mean, one minute you're changing a light bulb or whatever, and the next – smithereens."

Meredith put down her fork. "Accidents happen all the time. It just takes a moment. People are pretty fragile. That's why Dad and I worry so much about you and your sister." She paused. "Did you hear it was an accident?"

Maggie gulped some juice. "Sure, I guess. What else would it be?"

It was nice to be young, Meredith thought, and for more reasons than the gusto with which Maggie licked the syrup off her fork. "So, I might be a few minutes late tonight," she said. "Do you want me to see if Shawna can keep you guys company?" .

"No, thanks. We'll be fine. You'll make dinner, right?"

"Sure." Meredith was a little surprised. Usually, Maggie and Lucy jumped at the chance to be with their stepmother of three years, the annoyingly pert, blonde, and fun Mrs. Dr. Alexander Bennett. "Everything okay with Shawna?"

"Yeah." Maggie paused. "I was thinking, Mom. People can't help who they fall in love with, right? I mean, I don't think they can – love just happens, and then you just have to go with it, right?"

Oh, my. Maggie was growing up. Translation: are Daddy and Shawna responsible for having an affair and leaving us, or was it just an accident? Or, even

18

worse, did they do it deliberately, to be mean? Or, more romantically, was it fate? Maggie was, of course, sad when her parents got divorced, but as far as Meredith knew, she had never considered the situation from a moral perspective. And, as much as Alex had rocked her world by leaving her, and despite her continuing – affection -- for him, Meredith had always tried to avoid casting aspersions on Shawna and their marriage, at least in front of Maggie and Lucy. Her children had to have a good relationship with these people. They were all family now.

"It's complicated, Honey. I guess it depends on the situation." Maggie glared at her. "Okay, what do I think? Falling in love is a decision that has a lot of emotion in it – but it's still a decision. I think people are making a choice, and they are responsible for it, even if that choice has a lot of – chemistry involved. Well, then – all set?" she asked brightly, surveying Maggie's clean plate.

"Yes. Ugh, I have math this afternoon. I wonder what kind of weird sub we'll have, with Mrs. Block gone for good."

And life goes on, Meredith thought, picking up her purse, even after a spectacular calamity.

Wedged onto the beige living room couch between Lauren and Great Aunt Ida, Mindy Steinmetz idly kicked her foot and tried not to look bored. She felt her previous heroic determination to stick by her best friend dwindling. It had been a long, miserable day, and Lauren's old geezer relatives were swarming all over the house like cockroaches in the dark. What Lauren really needed was to lie down on her flowered bedspread next to Mindy, listen to her Alanis Morissette cassette, and just chill. Unfortunately, theater-person cousin Tracy had snatched Lauren's hand and was now gazing soulfully into her eyes.

"I am so, so sorry, Lauren. Aunt Marcia was totally my favorite aunt. If there is anything I can do…."

Yeah, right, Mindy thought, you two are so close. Like, I have never heard of you before, and I bet you are in the chorus of "A Corny Old Musical" at Someplace Lame High in Lima, Ohio. You've probably seen Aunt Marcia a total of three times, at family weddings where she said hi, politely asked about school, and then moved on to someone she actually knew.

Mostly I'll remember Mrs. Block asking if I needed a ride home, Mindy thought, and the back of her head driving me. The North Shore had two types of moms. Type One wanted to be best teenage girl buddies with their daughters' friends. They were always inviting you over for dinner and trying to hang out with you. This was a little weird, since they wanted to be cool and were not, and sometimes they confided things you totally did not want to know. But they could provide perks, like the odd beer or family trip to Cabo. Type Two was either scared of teenagers or bored by them. If a kid were standing around in her kitchen, these moms would back away slowly, as if they were meeting a grizzly bear on a hike. Despite being a junior high teacher, and therefore familiar with random teens, Mrs. Block was a Type Two. Maybe it was a math thing.

"Lauren," Mindy said, grabbing her arm and raising her eyebrows to signal a rescue attempt, "do you want something to eat?"

"No thanks, I couldn't. You go ahead."

Okay, fine, Mindy had about had it up to here, as her grandpa used to say. She hadn't eaten all day, and she was starving. This grandpa, who used to be Orthodox, had told her that Judaism prescribes certain foods after a parent dies. You aren't supposed to eat much right away, just a boiled egg with some ashes on it or something, because that's really all you can stomach anyway. Gradually, after a week or so, you work up to matzo ball soup. This is just another example of the amazing wisdom of Judaism, like not eating rats during the bubonic plague. But nobody here seemed to know that. The extended family was fressing away in the dining room, where every square inch of the table was covered with lox and lasagna. It was almost enough to make you sick, even if you already weren't. Mindy placed a slice of cheese, a carrot stick, and a cookie on a paper plate, positioned herself in a corner, and began nibbling.

The front door opened, admitting a familiar chocolate linen dress and unmistakable profusion of red hair, like a hot fudge sundae with a frizzy cherry on top. That would be her mother. Because Susie was also a Type Two, Mindy was surprised to see her. She had probably realized that it would be bad form to sit in the car and honk. Swiveling around to survey her options, Susie sported an appropriate solemn expression while brandishing a pie tin like a shield. With obvious relief, she spotted her daughter.

"Oh, good. Once I find a place to set down this quiche, we can leave. Boy, there's a lot of food. Maybe I should just put it in the kitchen," Susie said. "Where is it?"

"I don't know, Mom."

"What do you mean, you don't know. You've been here a million times," said Susie, squeezing through a doorway toward the back of the house. Her mother might be short, but she was fast.

"Hello." Ron Block stood positioned in the next doorway. Behind him, a Subzero refrigerator masqueraded as a cherry armoire.

"I brought you a quiche," Susie announced, blushing. "I mean, I'm so sorry. I'm Mindy's mother. We met this morning, but I don't know if you would remember."

"I remember," he said. "Thank you for the food. You can just give it to me." He put out his hands.

"Oh, no, that's all right, I don't want to be any trouble. I'll just put it in the kitchen."

Firmly blocking her way, Ron took hold of the quiche. "It's no trouble. It was kind of you to come by. And to lend us Mindy. I know she helped Lauren a lot today. She's a lovely girl." He turned and smiled at Mindy, who grinned back warily. Mr. Block had ignored her for four years. Had grief turned him into someone friendly, or was he up to something?

Well, Susie was buying it. "We're glad to help however we can. I know what it's like to lose a spouse," she confided. "I mean, I know what you're going through."

"Mom!" said Mindy.

"What do you mean?" asked Ron.

22

"Maybe Mindy has told you – my husband Joel has cancer." Susie looked down at the floor. "I know it's not the exact same thing…."

"Obviously," muttered Mindy.

"But it is scary, and it does make you think."

"I'm sure," said Ron. "I'm sorry."

"He is supposed to get better," Susie said, looking at Mindy. "But you never know."

"Mom!" said Mindy.

"Well, I certainly will be hoping for good things for you and your family," said Ron.

"Thank you," said Susie. "It was nice finally meeting you. I think I'll take Mindy home now. I'm sure everyone is tired."

"Yes," said Ron. "I do think we need to wind this up and get some rest."

"Good night, Mr. Block. Please tell Lauren I'll call her tomorrow," said Mindy.

"Good night." Ron walked into the kitchen with the quiche.

"What a nice man," said Susie to her daughter as they walked out the front door onto the stone steps.

"I guess." He had never seemed that nice before. Maybe his wife's death had changed him, at least for today.

Leaving work a tad early, Meredith drove up Green Bay Road toward Glencoe and Marcia Block's shiva. As a mother who had spoken with Mrs. Block for only five minutes in her life and as a North Shore prosecutor, she didn't belong there. But, hey, Ron had

23

invited everyone at the funeral. And the more she thought about it, the more she wanted to pop in and check out the scene. The woman had died falling through a glass table! She couldn't just let this one go.

Just north of tiny downtown Glencoe, Meredith turned east onto Maple Hill Road. Life was good on this dream block, large brick houses scattered along an unraveling spool of green lawns and flowering trees, sandwiched between the train tracks to Chicago and the lake. She parked near a horseshoe gravel driveway bursting with Mercedes and BMW's, like a luxury hotel touting its clientele. The Block manse, a center entrance colonial, continued horizontally like a stutter, yards and yards of red brick wall. A white-columned portico stood sentry, as did Alarms Unlimited, according to the medallion planted in the front garden. Unfortunately, thought Meredith, nothing outside could protect the Block family from itself.

Well, it's a shiva, come on in, she thought, throwing open the front door and stepping into an impressive, chandelier-lit two-story foyer. To her right, an immense living room of the museum variety – used only for law firm recruiting dinners and the odd post mortem -- displayed tasteful neutral furniture, abstract paintings -- black slashes and brown scratching – and a white Steinway tossed in the corner like a forgotten handkerchief. A few mourners perched on the couches and chairs, but most milled about, chatting and noshing on snacks or sipping chardonnay. To Meredith's left, a crowd packed a dining room much like George Washington's, if Martha had piled their footed table with bagels and smoked sable. Meredith wondered where the family actually spent its time – probably in an old sunroom in the back, watching a giant TV from a pizza-stained couch, or in the requisite gourmet kitchen, heating leftovers in the microwave. For starters, she would like to see that kitchen. It might be the scene of the crime.

Nudging her way to the kitchen doorway, Meredith spied a massive granite island festooned with hanging copper pots, like ornaments on a Christmas tree. Ron Block emerged and positioned himself directly in her path. He had the matinee-idol good looks and oily charm of an up-market anchorman, but he filled the opening like a giant starfish.

"Hello," he said. "Welcome to my home."

"Thank you," Meredith replied, extending her hand toward one of his tentacles. "I'm Meredith Bennett. My daughter Maggie is – was – one of your wife's students. I wanted to express my condolences." This was not strictly true, but she couldn't really say, "just snooping." And she was sorry that Mrs. Block had died. "I hope you don't mind, I'd like to get a drink of water."

She could see that he did mind, but Ron's height and lack of basketball experience worked against him. When a slovenly uncle slopping red wine momentarily distracted him, Meredith slipped under his arm and rushed forward. To save time, she skipped the water charade and hurried past the cherry cabinets and professional grade ovens to the breakfast area.

There was no table. Four chairs pushed against the wall left only a gaping absence, like a room holding its breath. Above, a ceiling fan with an attached light fixture spun tepidly, perhaps to dispel the faint scent of cleaning products. Below lay a hard travertine floor. A cordless phone on a built-in desk stood at least ten feet from the eating area.   On the other side of the bay window, the world was sunny, the lawn greening, the sky a perfect Wedgewood blue.   Tulip clusters, landscaped splashes of pink and yellow and lavender, burst from the border as if tossed like confetti by the Goddess of Spring.

"What is this about?" asked Ron.   "I've been through a lot. I don't need this. My wife died here. Please."

"I'm sorry," said Meredith, turning to face him. He looked ashen, exhausted. How had she missed this? His open plea surprised and shamed her. What was she thinking, coming here tonight? This man's wife was dead. The police had concluded that it was an accident. She should not be playing games with him. "I am the mother of a student. But I am also an assistant state's attorney."

"You have a lot of nerve, coming here tonight. I'm going to have to ask you to leave." Ron was calm, but he had raised his voice. She needed to extricate herself before the crowd came after her with torches and pitchforks.

"You're right, said Meredith, "this was out of line. But your wife's death was strange. We're both lawyers, you get that, right? And I knew her, a little bit. And my daughter knew her, she liked her. I just wanted to chat with you for a moment, just to erase any -- lingering concerns. Would you be willing to meet me, to talk with me tomorrow – you and your daughter -- just for a few minutes?"

"So, you barge in here and ask me to do you the favor of putting myself and my daughter in legal jeopardy the day after we bury my wife and her mother?"

"That's it, yes," said Meredith.

"Forget it," said Ron. "Read the police report, and leave us alone." He turned and walked out of the kitchen.

Heading for the front door through the living room, Meredith noticed Lauren Block resting on the couch near the fireplace. She was one of those amazing young women who always look perfectly put together – silky blunt-cut hair, neat crisp blouse, pearl-buttoned cardigan – no matter the scene or her inner state of dishabille. The crowd was beginning to clear. Meredith scanned the room for Ron – he hadn't followed her -- and then sat down.

"Lauren?" she said. "I'm Mrs. Bennett. I'm very sorry for your loss."

"Thank you," Lauren replied automatically.

"Look, I'm a lawyer, I work for the state. I know you already talked to the police, but I would really like to talk with you about your mother's death. Not now, but maybe tomorrow?"

Lauren straightened up in her seat. "Could I talk to you alone – without my dad?" she asked.

"Are you eighteen years old?"

"Yes," said Lauren.

"Then, yes," said Meredith. "Here's my card."

"I'll come by in the afternoon," said Lauren, slipping it under a seat cushion. "Don't tell my dad."

"No problem," said Meredith. "See you tomorrow afternoon."

She got up and walked to the front door. Whistling would have been bad form, but she felt like doing it. She would get details from the Glencoe police in the morning, and in the afternoon she would talk with Lauren Block. Her chutzpah had paid off. She glanced back at the Block dining room, bursting with casseroles and vegetable trays, but she wasn't the least bit tempted. It was time to go home to her own daughters and rustle up some scrambled eggs.

Chapter Three

May 2, 1997

The next morning, Meredith parked in front of Glencoe Village Hall, a white-columned, red brick building surprisingly similar to the Block house, with the addition of a clock tower and three giant doors for fire engines. The Village Hall housed the Department of Public Safety, a combination of police officers, firefighters, and paramedics dedicated to helping Glencoe residents. Seated across from Officer Abby Anderson, Meredith wondered if these community aides possessed the necessary cynicism to consider the possibility that Ron Block had deliberately offed his wife. Abby's blonde bob brushed the shoulders of her short-sleeved navy uniform as she fished a file folder out of a stack on her desk.

"Yeah, I went to the Blocks' house Saturday morning. I'll never forget it. Blood everywhere, and the girl was freaking out. Not your usual a.m. here on the North Shore." Abby stirred powdered creamer into a Botanic Gardens mug of coffee and handed Meredith the folder.

"Thanks, Abby, I appreciate it. I know you guys have determined this was an accident. I just need to prove it to myself."

"You knew the lady, I get it. I'd be the same way." She tapped her blonde head with her index finger. "You can't turn it off."

"Yup. And this was such a weird way to die. How did Ron Block seem, when you showed up?"

"Very distressed, distraught, you might say." Abby shook her head. "It was horrible. He did everything right, called 911 immediately, he tried to help her. But she just bled out right in front of him. Freaky, I agree with you. We felt terrible for him."

"What did the autopsy report say? Any unusual wounds, anything in Marcia's system?"

"You mean like, did he stab her a few extra times after she was down? I don't think so. All the wounds appeared to be glass cuts consistent with her fall. She'd eaten some breakfast, but that's about it. No alcohol. We didn't ask for a tox screen, it wasn't necessary."

"Did you get statements from Ron and Lauren?"

"We did," said Abby. "We felt bad about it, but we wanted to be thorough."

"And how did you get the statements?" asked Meredith. "Did you bring Ron and Lauren here?"

"Yeah," said Abby. "We thought it would be best to get them out of the house. We put them in a room in the back and told them to state what happened in their own words. We asked a few questions to prompt them."

"Were they together?"

"Yes." Abby flushed. "Mr. Block wouldn't leave his daughter. She really was a mess. An emotional mess, I mean. He had blood all over him at the house, so we let him change before he came in. I noticed that he had sustained a few cuts himself, so we had a paramedic patch him up. There was a lot of glass, and he was crawling around, trying to stop her bleeding."

"Okay, thanks, Abby. I'll give these back to you when I'm done." Meredith settled back in her chair with Ron Block's police statement.

My name is Ronald Block. I live at 213 Maple Hill Road with my wife Marcia and my daughter Lauren. I am fifty-nine years old. I am a bankruptcy lawyer at Eagles & Fitch in Chicago. Marcia is – was – fifty-five. She taught seventh grade math at Wilmette Junior High School. We have been married for twenty-four years. Lauren is our only child. She is eighteen and a senior at New Trier High School.

This morning started like any other Saturday. Marcia and I got up, got dressed, made our own breakfasts. After we ate and read the paper, Marcia noticed a spider on the kitchen ceiling. I told her I would get it in a minute, but I needed to check my messages from work. It was around 9:30 in the morning, and I hadn't checked since the night before. I picked up the kitchen phone, and I was wandering around, listening and responding to messages. After a few minutes, I noticed that Marcia had set up the ladder next to the kitchen table. She climbed it and started swatting at the ceiling. I figured she was handling it, and I continued working. The next thing I knew, I heard a little yelp, and then a crash. Marcia must have lost her footing, and she fell through the glass table.

I went to her right away. She was bleeding a lot, and I was upset, I didn't know what to do. You just start shaking, you know, and you can't think straight, but you know you have to do something, everything depends on you. I must have been yelling, because Lauren came down too. She had been asleep upstairs, you know how teenagers are. There was so much blood, but at the same time, I couldn't believe that it was so serious, that she might actually die. I mean, we'd just been eating cereal, for Christ's sake. Anyway, I realized I had the phone in my hand, and I called 911. Then I got on the floor with Marcia and some dish towels, and I tried to stop the bleeding. I was pressing on some spots, but the towels were just soaking through, and I didn't know if there might still be glass in the wounds.

The ambulance came, and the police, and the firemen, everybody. The paramedics put Marcia in the ambulance. They worked as fast as they could, they were very professional, but I could tell they didn't have much hope. A police woman drove me and Lauren to Evanston Hospital. By the time we got there, Marcia had passed away.

Marcia and I had a great marriage. We were looking forward to being empty nesters, being able to spend more time together. We were close, best friends, all that. I can't believe she is gone.

Meredith turned the page to Lauren's statement.

My name is Lauren Block. I live at 213 Maple Hill Road in Glencoe with my parents, Ron and Marcia Block. I am a senior at New Trier High School.

On Saturday morning, I was sleeping late, since there's no school, and I was really tired. I didn't hear anything until my dad started shouting, and then I got out of bed and went into the kitchen. My mother was lying on the floor, and my dad was standing a little away, he might have been on the phone. There was so much blood, all over the floor, it was awful. But my mom saw me come in, and she got all panicky. She told me to stay back, she didn't want me to cut my feet on the glass. She always did that, glasses would break on the stone floor, and she always sent me out right away so I wouldn't get hurt. So I couldn't go up to her, I couldn't tell her that I loved her, anything. The paramedics took her away, and she died in the ambulance with them.

The police let me get dressed and they let dad change, and then they drove us to the hospital. Afterwards, we were going to go home, but they took us here instead. I didn't want to go home anyway. I didn't want to see what the kitchen looked like.

My parents got along fine, like any parents. Dad worked a lot, and Mom worked too, but on a teacher's schedule, so she could take care of me. It was a pretty nice life, until today.

Meredith put the statements down on the desk. It was heartbreaking, a full life ended in a moment, based on a fluky decision and a simple misstep. It happened every day, and all the what-ifs would follow, the family beating themselves up. What if he had squashed the spider, what if she had gotten up earlier, what if they had bought a wooden table? What if they had slept in or gone out for breakfast or, for one blinking Shabbat, he had saved his work calls until Sunday? Then Marcia would be explaining the multiplication of fractions to a class of bored seventh graders, instead of six feet under the willow tree in a cemetery in Skokie.

"Thanks, Abby. Did Ron give his statement first?"

"He did. He wanted to, and that was fine with us." She had finished her coffee and was shuffling through papers in another file.

"Is there anything else you can tell me? Any previous contact with the family, anything that seemed odd to you?"

"No, nothing." She shook her head. "They were just an ordinary family. Shit happens, I guess." Abby picked up the statements and opened the Block folder.

"It certainly does," said Meredith. "One last thing. Could I have copies of those statements? And thanks so much for your help."

Lauren tromped toward the information desk in the lobby of the Skokie Courthouse like a convict marching to the executioner. The reek of popcorn from the newsstand sickened her, and she realized that, although it was now afternoon, she hadn't eaten today. Her mother's voice in her head urged her to try a little something, maybe a cracker, but she just couldn't. How could she eat when her mother was dead, and she had to rat out her father for killing her?

While Lauren waited, the woman at the circular desk flirted with a loitering security guard. "Excuse me," said Lauren. "Excuse me!"

The woman swiveled toward her. "Well?"

"I'm looking for Meredith Bennett's office? She's a state's attorney?" Lauren smoothed her skirt and tugged her cardigan into place. Blessed with her mother's sleek hair and almond eyes, she looked like a well-groomed Persian cat.

Spilling out of her red blouse, the information lady made a great show of shuffling the laminated pages of a loose leaf notebook. "Upstairs," she pronounced, slamming the book shut and shifting her padded hips back toward the guard.

"But where exactly?"

The woman ignored her. After giving the desk a petulant kick noisy enough to get the guard's attention, Lauren turned and hurried up the stairs. At the top, she hesitated. She was exhausted, she hadn't slept, people were horrible, it was all too much. A motherly woman in a gray pantsuit approached and put out her hand.

"Lauren, I'm so glad you came. I'm sure yesterday was a blur. I'm Meredith Bennett. Please, follow me." Meredith touched her shoulder and turned back, opening the door to a green carpeted hallway and ushering her into a windowless cubicle.

"How did you know I was here?" asked Lauren.

"Barb buzzed me. I know, she's an acquired taste." Meredith smiled. "Please, sit down. Can I get you something – a glass of water, hot tea?"

"No, thanks."

Settling behind a desk overflowing with accordion folders, Meredith gazed at her with attention and concern. Lauren started to cry. "Lauren, I am so sorry for your loss." Meredith pushed a box of Kleenex toward her and waited.

Lauren blinked and blotted her nose. "I'm sorry, I know you're busy. It's just – I needed to tell someone, in case it's important." She sat straight but averted her eyes. "I don't really know anything. I don't want to get my father in trouble."

"Just tell me what happened. I have plenty of time," said Meredith.

"Well, I Didn't See Anything." Lauren spoke emphatically. "And, I mean, how could it have been anything but an accident? I mean, who would push somebody off a step ladder and think it would kill them?"

"Okay. But something is bothering you. What is it?"

"It's just that – they'd been fighting." Lauren stared at her knees.

"Your mother and father. Before she fell?"

"Yes. And other times too."

"And you could hear them from your room?"

"I could hear their raised voices. I could hear him – lecturing her."

"Do you have any idea what the fight was about?" Meredith asked.

"They really didn't get along that well. They didn't really – I don't know – smile at each other much. They seemed uncomfortable. I could tell my father thought my mother was – I don't know, less, unimportant. Like a secretary, or a waitress. Just the way he talked to her. She was a teacher, a mom, and he was a big deal lawyer. I guess he is a big deal, he makes a lot of money. She picked at him. She said he worked too much, and she always worried that he wanted someone prettier, someone younger. He did work a lot, but I never knew about any – affair. I don't think that could have happened – he was so old, and really pretty boring. I don't think he was interested in that sort of thing, he just liked to talk about, I don't know, liquidity."

"Was your father ever violent? Did he ever hit your mother?"

"Oh, no, nothing like that. If he had any feelings, he kept them pretty controlled. I really can't imagine it."

"Maybe you can imagine it, though. You were worried enough to come here today."

"It's just – they were fighting, and then she died." She started to cry again. "What if he finally lost his temper? What if he gave her a push? Maybe he didn't mean anything by it. But what if he did?"

"Lauren, are you afraid for your own safety?"

Lauren recoiled. "No, of course not. If he did anything, I'm sure it was impulsive. Anyway, my father doesn't care enough about me to kill me.

Meredith reached across her desk to touch the fragile, disintegrating girl. "Lauren, I want you to listen carefully to me. Married people fight. You know that, don't you? Your parents were married a long time, right?"

"Yes," she sniffed.

"Okay. A long marriage will have ups and downs. Your parents were in a down. They were fighting, and they may both have been unhappy. That doesn't mean they didn't love each other, and that certainly doesn't mean your father doesn't love you. Sometimes fathers – parents -- work a lot, sometimes they are remote or preoccupied, but they still love their families. Maybe this horrible situation will be a wake-up call for your dad, and you will get closer."

"Maybe," Lauren muttered. She straightened and looked Meredith in the eyes. "But what if he killed my mom?"

"That would be terrible, and he should be punished – if that were true," said Meredith. "That would be my job. So you were smart to come to me. If he did push her, though, it would be very hard to prove, even if they were fighting. Maybe your mother was upset during the argument, and she lost her balance. That could have happened too. I want you to think very hard. Is there anything specific that makes you think he may have killed her? Anything he has ever said or done, or that your mother told you, or that you heard or saw that morning?"

"No. Just the arguing." Lauren shook her head and wiped her nose with a tissue.

"All right. If that changes, if you think of anything more, or if you find out anything more, will you please call me?"

"Yes." Lauren rested back in her chair. She looked relieved.

"Would you like that glass of water now? And maybe a cookie? I think there might be one in the coffee room."

"I don't want to be any trouble."

"It's no trouble at all. You just stay here a minute."

Meredith went to the coffee room. She found two cookies and a carton of orange juice. It looked like a snack for someone who had donated blood. She walked back and presented them to Lauren.

"Thank you," said Lauren gratefully, putting out her hands. "I feel a little better now. My mother used to give me cookies and juice after school, when I was a little girl. I think this is exactly what I need." She nibbled a cookie, drank a sip of juice, and then she left.

Drying her hands on a dish towel, Meredith approached the ringing phone. Expecting a telemarketer, she picked up the receiver like a slimy bit of refuse and muttered a disgruntled hello.

"Meredith? It's Alex."

"Oh, yes, sorry, hello. It's me." After ten years of marriage, his departure for younger pastures, and four years of a surprisingly amicable divorce, Alex's sudden appearance still unnerved her. "What's up?"

"Well, I need to talk to you about something. Can I come over for a few minutes?"

"Sure. When would you like to come by?"

"Is now okay? I don't have to work tonight."

"Um, sure. That would be fine." Meredith was wearing a thinning University of Chicago tee shirt listing all of their affiliated Nobel Prize winners and a pilling cardigan, complementing her forty-two-year-old face and post-dinner teeth. As she hurried to the bathroom to at least wash up, the doorbell rang.

"That was fast," she observed, opening the front door to the grim-faced, but still attractive, Dr. Alexander Bennett. His lanky frame, square jaw, and magnified eyes might not be a cheerleader's ticket to heaven, but he always made Meredith a little runny around the edges.

"Sorry. We were on our way back from dinner."

Alex's wife Shawna stepped out from behind him and waved. "Hiya. I hope we're not interrupting anything," she said, flipping her blonde hair and blinking her blank eyes. Like Meredith, Shawna was wearing jeans, but the effect was different -- like the skin of a long-stemmed fruit, topped with a short gold and white sleeveless tank top flashing just an inch of taut tummy. Meredith's heart sank as it always did when faced with the babe who had kidnapped her husband's nether regions, which were unfortunately connected to the rest of him. There was no way she could compete with this. And yet, Alex missed Meredith. At least, that's what he said. Well, too little too late, she thought weakly, giving her baggy butt a pathetic shake.

"Hello, Shawna. This is a surprise." Meredith ushered them into her Wilmette split-level, a material come-down from the luxurious Kenilworth house she had shared with Alex, but her very own home, just right for a family of three. She pointed her guests to the brown couch she had chosen for its stain-resistant fabric and sat herself in the corduroy chair where she could read or gather her wits while Maggie and Lucy watched TV in the den behind the kitchen, as they were doing now.

"We couldn't wait to tell you – we have exciting news!" Shawna flashed her dazzling teeth, surrounded by slick pink lip gloss.

Meredith's heart contracted, and she took a deep breath. She knew this day had to arrive, despite the fact that Alex sometimes seemed to want to come back to her and their daughters. Shawna was young, and she was alone all day, long days while Alex worked at the hospital. Step aerobics could take even Shawna only so far as a meaningful life purpose. It was natural, and Meredith would have to bear it. And it wasn't as if Meredith had rushed into Alex's arms and welcomed him back. She wasn't ready for that, and she wasn't sure he was either – that was part of the problem. She didn't know if Alex was a man who had left her and learned from his mistake, or if he was a serial wife-dumper. And now it was too late.

"I got a fellowship, Meredith. It's for a year, down at …."

"It's in Orlando!" injected Shawna. She could not stop grinning. "We're going to Florida for a year, together!"

"Yes," said Alex. He tried to grab Meredith's eyes. "It's at Orlando Medical Center. I'll be able to do the research I've been hoping to pursue."

"I'm surprised," Meredith said, playing for time. This was not what she had expected, and she was trying to decide if it was better or worse. "You never mentioned that you were applying for a fellowship."

"I didn't want to upset – the girls – until I knew it was happening." His long legs jutted under the coffee table, and he leaned toward her chair. "I thought maybe getting away would be good for us," he said.

Meredith folded her arms over her chest. She wasn't sure which "us" he meant. Shawna tilted her chin toward Meredith. "We want some time alone, he means. We've never really had it. We love Maggie and Lucy. But – we need some time alone. With just our family. Us."

"I'm sorry you feel that way," Meredith said steadily. "The girls will miss you."

"I will miss them too. But I have to keep my priorities straight."

Meredith turned to Alex. "And how do your daughters fit into your priorities?" she asked.

They heard scuffling in the kitchen, and Maggie and Lucy walked into the room.

"I knew it was you!" said Lucy, tripping over her father's legs to perch between Shawna and Alex.

"What's going on?" asked Maggie. She stood beside her mother's chair, her dark eyes shifting between Shawna and her father. Meredith took her arm.

"Dad has a chance to do some important research. That's the good news." She was not going to sugarcoat this. Maggie was too smart. "The bad news, for us, is that he and Shawna will be moving to Orlando for a year. Just for one year," she said, looking at Alex. He nodded.

"Yes, just for one year," said Alex. "Then we will come back." Meredith could feel Maggie's muscles tense.

"We can visit you," offered Lucy, caution replacing her normal exuberance as she absorbed the mood in the room.

"Yes, of course," said Shawna. "But not for a while."

"What do you mean?" asked Maggie.

"She just means that we will need to get settled, and you will have a lot of things to do here. You won't want to visit in the summer, it's way too hot, and then school starts, and you'll be busy," said Alex. He had thought about this.

Her eyes filling, Maggie looked at Meredith. "Mom?"

"We could come for Thanksgiving," suggested Lucy. "We could go to Disney. That would be perfect."

"They do have the whole week off then. I think it would be good if we had a plan," Meredith said firmly, pushing back the prospect of her own solitary Thanksgiving. She could have both drumsticks, and a bottle of vodka.

"Okay," said Alex. "Let's do that." He stood up.

"When are you leaving?" Meredith asked.

"Soon," said Shawna. "We're going to rent a furnished house down there. It shouldn't be hard. Then we'll just pack our bikinis, and we're off!"

"I'll be in touch," said Alex. He walked up to Maggie and gave her a stiff hug. "It will go fast," he said. "I love you."

"Right," said Maggie. "I can tell."

Shawna gave Lucy a peck on the cheek. "We'll say goodbye before we go," she offered.

"Please do," said Meredith.

She opened the front door and saw them out. Then the Bennett girls retreated to their respective bedrooms to cry for a bit. They needed to absorb the shock. They could discuss it after that.

Chapter Four

June 1997

Sweating on the bleachers of Northwestern University's basketball arena, Joel Steinmetz gave his wife Susie a cranky little shove. It was her fault that he was sitting here, a full hour before New Trier High School's graduation ceremony was scheduled to begin. She was sure that the place would be packed with Type A parents anxious to see their extra-special progeny cross the stage for their three seconds of glory, and she was right, of course. Although the doors had opened only fifteen minutes before they arrived, delayed by Mindy's petulant battle with her homemade updo, they were relegated to the upper tier of some very hard and sticky metal bleachers. Joel imagined a river of sweat coursing down his neck, under his button-down shirt, and into the port implanted in his chest to allow oncology nurses easy access to his circulatory system.

"Well, it's a good thing we got here when we did. Just look at all the people coming in now. Where do they think they're going to sit?" Susie wrinkled her nose at the relative latecomers as if sniffing something slightly off, like milk a day after its sell-by date.

"I don't think it matters, it's not like we're close," said Joel testily. "I hope I make it through this thing. I can't believe we have to listen to a thousand names."

"Oh, cut it out, you're such a grump." Susie scowled at him, a red storm cloud in a lacy white blouse and flowered skirt she had bought for the occasion on sale at Saks. Her frosted nails scanned the tremendously long list of almost graduates. "Look, here's Mindy's name!"

"Yup, it's a miracle. And in two and a half hours, we'll hear the principal mispronounce it."

"Not the principal, the Senior Girls' Advisor Chair. I'm not even going to talk to you," Susie said, swiveling sideways.

At least Joel was at the end of an aisle, with Susie on his left and a parade of steamy parents coursing up the stairs on his other side. A multigenerational family wearing sailboat sportswear had filled in their row from the other side, leaving one forlorn empty seat next to Susie. The mother in that group seemed to know everyone else in the arena. Half-standing, she waved significantly at expensively dressed adults above, below, and to either side of the Steinmetz's, like the Queen on a cruise ship. Joel felt like he was in the middle of a Druid shunning ritual, if there were such a thing.

"I remember a time when you would have been excited to be here," Susie continued, immediately reneging on her threat.

"Yeah, well, I remember a time I didn't have cancer," he said. That sounded childish even to Joel. "You're right," he tried. "I'm lucky to be here. Who

46

knows how many more life cycle events I'll be able to attend?"

Susie absorbed herself in her program, but Joel knew, after eighteen years of marriage, that she was studiously ignoring him. Yes, they had been married eighteen years, with an eighteen-year-old daughter to show for it. It was a shotgun wedding, although in this case, the groom was the man holding the gun. Susie had been a twenty-four year old receptionist at the AA Ants Away Pest Control Company, where Joel, a thirty-one year old insecticide prodigy, managed a staff of pest control specialists and wheedled his red-headed assistant into the back seat of his truck on every possible occasion. A Boston University French major, Susie was clearly meant for better things. But Joel was persuasive, and he had no condoms. He was lucky she had married him. And now, their Mindy, who had won him the brass ring and a passably contented home life right up until he was diagnosed with colon cancer, was about to fly the nest. Leaving two old birds, one molting, one spreading her tail feathers, staring at each other.

A small orchestra of New Trier juniors began to play "Pomp and Circumstance" surprisingly well. Susie began to cry.

"Come on, Old Girl, it's all right. Tomorrow she'll be leaving dishes in her bedroom as usual." Joel patted Susie's knee.

"I know, it's just – this is a milestone." Susie scrounged in her purse for a Kleenex and blew her nose.

"A few stragglers still coming in," snorted Joel, jealously wishing that he hadn't been sitting here for forty-five minutes. His back was already sore. He switched his bottom from cheek to cheek.

"Look, isn't that Ron Block?" asked Susie, scooting forward to check out a handsome man anxiously surveying the arena.

"Beats me, I never met the guy. Some nerve, showing up now, and thinking he can sit somewhere."

"Well, he doesn't have a wife to let him know how these things work, does he? We should be nice to him. Ron!" Susie shouted out, waving her arms.

Ron thought he heard his name, but that seemed unlikely. He doubted he knew more than a handful of the two thousand parents looming over him, taking up every available seat. But the orchestra was playing, and if he didn't find a place fast, he was going to find himself receiving a second high school diploma.

"Ron, up here!"

He heard the cry again and scanned the crowd. There, in the middle section, not in an ideal spot, but in an area where there might still be oxygen, a small flame-haired woman in a bright skirt was jumping around and waving in his direction. It must be that mom, Lauren's friend Mindy's mother, Mrs. – uh – he had no idea. Where was Marcia, he needed her today. She would have managed Lauren's décolletage crisis, gotten them here early, and known Mindy's mother's name. Now that Mrs. Mindy had called attention to him, everyone here was probably buzzing. "Isn't that the guy whose wife fell through the glass table? How did that happen? Seems kind of weird...." Ron hurried up the steps toward Mrs. Mindy, who was waving so frantically that he feared another catastrophe.

"Hello," he said.

"Here!" the woman motioned. "We saved you a seat! Well, not really," she blushed, "but by some miracle it's open, and we'd love for you to join us."

"Thank you," he said, extending his hand toward the tired bald man stewing next to the aisle. "Ron Block. I'm Lauren's dad, on this occasion."

"Joel Steinmetz," said the bald man, standing to allow Ron to pass. Ron felt his legs brush the woman's as he scooted by her.

"I'm Susie," she said. "We met – before. You might not remember," she hurried.

"Susie," he said, making a mental note. "Thank you for rescuing me."

"Sure," she said, as he took his seat. She looked pretty, flushed from the heat. "Did you get a program?"

"No," he said, displaying empty hands, as the orchestra began another round.

"Here, you can have Joel's, he's not using it," she said, plucking the papers from her husband's lap and thrusting them at Ron. "Lauren's name is in there," she said. "Look, here they come!"

As the music crescendoed, the New Trier Class of 1997 filed into the arena -- boys in white tuxedos, black bow ties, and boutonnieres, escorting girls in white formal gowns, each carrying a single red rose. Ron checked the dais for a ravenous volcano but found only authority figures with benevolent looks plastered on their faces.

"At this rate it'll take an hour for them just to sit down," grumbled Joel, as Susie watched excitedly, her eyes brimming with tears.

"Look, here comes Lauren!" Susie said, grabbing Ron's arm. "She looks beautiful!"

Ron stared at Lauren. She did look beautiful. He still thought of her as a chubby little girl, but she wasn't, not anymore. While he was at the office, she had transformed into a sleek young woman, her shiny dark hair a striking contrast to her simple white dress. She glided down the aisle, her hand resting on her escort's arm. She looked like an elegant little doll. She looked like Marcia.

"I'm sorry," said Joel. "I have to leave for a minute. I need some air." His face was gray and gleaming with sweat. He stood unsteadily.

"I'll go with you," Ron said. Joel looked decidedly unwell, but Susie would not want to leave, she hadn't seen her own daughter yet. Marcia would have been the same way.

"No, I can go," said Susie uncertainly.

"I insist," said Ron, leaping up, as Joel stumbled down the stairs toward the floor of the arena.

They didn't quite make it. Joel vomited at the feet of a security guard monitoring the doorway through which the graduates were processing. A quick-thinking senior boy pushed a girl dressed like a vanilla cupcake to the sidelines, saving her hem and shoes from the sour mess. Ron helped Joel outside, where he completed his activities in a bush. Shakily, he reached for a tissue and wiped his mouth.

"Do you want to sit down?" asked Ron, gesturing toward a low cement wall. Joel sat, and Ron stood silent. It was nice to have a man helping him for a change, Joel thought. Susie was always running around yapping at him like a toy poodle. Ron just waited.

"It's the chemo," offered Joel. "I have cancer."

"It's too hot in there," said Ron.

"Northwestern should air condition it," Joel complained. "They have enough money."

"They probably don't use it much this time of year."

"Yeah, but they contract it out. Who cares if people are throwing up, as long as they get their money."

"That's business," said Ron.

"Have you ever been to a basketball game here?" asked Joel.

"No. Never had the chance. How about you?"

"I used to take Mindy when she was little. She liked the Wildcat and the popcorn. The games were terrible, but it was better for me than a Care Bears movie. She wouldn't go to any movie with me now."

"They're practically adults. I guess it's appropriate."

"Yeah," said Joel. "Hey, you can go back in if you want. I think I'll stay out here for a while. I have plenty of time before she gets her diploma. Being an 'S' and all."

"It's only high school graduation. I don't know what the big deal is," said Ron. "We expect them to graduate from high school."

"Agreed," said Joel. "But don't say that to Susie. I'm sure she's crying her eyes out in there."

"Where is Mindy going to college?" asked Ron.

"Indiana. It's pretty there, Bloomington. What about Lauren?"

"Skidmore."

"Oh, great school!" said Joel. He didn't know anything about it, but it sounded fancy. "You must be very proud."

"Oh, yeah," said Ron. "I know her mom was hoping for something better – you know, the Ivy League or something. She worked hard with Lauren for years, getting her tutors, pushing her to do her best."

"Yeah. Susie is a planner too. They just want the best for their kids."

"It's nice, though," said Ron. "The woman's touch. Especially with a daughter."

"Yeah," said Joel. "Umm, sorry…."

"Thanks," said Ron. "Maybe I'll go back in. Lauren is a 'B'. If you're okay."

"Sure, Buddy. Thanks again. Tell Susie I'll be in soon."

Ron turned and went back into the arena. No one had ever called him Buddy before. His life was changing, now that Marcia was gone. He went in to watch his daughter graduate. In a few months she would go to college, and he would be alone. It was a big deal, in a way.

"It was so nice of you to invite us here." Susie sipped a pink, fruity cocktail and smiled happily at Ron. She had looked pretty uptight when she walked into the Northmoor Country Club, but now that she was on her second drink, she was definitely relaxing. "Eating in a restaurant is tricky on graduation night. I mean, you want to celebrate, but you never know exactly when your reservation should be, and it gets so crowded and hectic."

"I'm glad you could join us," said Ron. He nodded his head toward their waiter. "Let's have a bottle of champagne for the table, please."

"Certainly, Mr. Block."

Mindy looked around suspiciously. She had been friends with Lauren for four years, and she had never eaten with her dad. He basically lived at work, and the Blocks weren't the sort of people who invited their daughter's friends to go out for dinner with them anyway. This place was stuffy and weird, a lot of brown velvet and creepy padded chairs with curly arms, and chandeliers with mini lamp shades over mini light bulbs. Maybe this was a style, like colonial. It was probably supposed to look classy, but Mindy thought it just looked old.

On the other hand, the waiters knew Mr. Block's name, which was kind of cool, and she really didn't want to go to Maggiano's in her long graduation dress, that would have been awkward. She could cheer Lauren up too, not maroon her with a bunch of geezers. The guy eating at the next table was seriously a hundred and three. He had a Filipino chick with him who kept wiping his mouth and checking his oxygen tank. It was depressing, and Lauren did not need that.

"Just give the girls a taste," said Ron, as the waiter uncorked the bottle with a festive pop. "I hope you don't mind," he said, turning to her parents. "Not strictly kosher, but one of the perks of membership."

Mindy sipped her bubbly drink. It was pretty good. After dinner she and Lauren would go to New Trier's graduation party, sponsored by freaked-out parents praying that the possibility of door prizes would keep the Class of 1997 from drinking themselves blind

53

and driving into a tree. Mindy had heard that a graduate won a VW Beetle last year, but she was not sure this was strictly true.

Finally the waiter brought some rolls and butter. Starving after the endless ceremony, Mindy sat hopeless as the bread basket languished next to her father. Joel didn't look very chipper, and he hadn't touched his drink. Susie, blithely ignoring him, was chatting away with Ron.

"This is a lovely place," she smiled. "Do you play tennis, Ron?"

Oh my god. Embarrassing even on an ordinary day, Susie was really pushing it tonight. "Dad," Mindy stage-whispered, "do you want a roll?"

"No thanks," he said. He did not take the hint.

Susie looked over. "Oh my goodness," she said, plucking the basket from the table and daintily fishing out a miniature croissant. "How special. Ron?" She passed the rolls to her host. Finally it was on its way around the table. Lauren received it from her father and quickly gave it to Mindy.

"You sure, Lauren?" she asked, grabbing a large, squishy bun from the top.

Always thin, Lauren had gotten skinny over the last month, since her mother died. Mindy tried to ply her with milkshakes and late night pizzas, but Lauren would just take a bite and leave the rest. In the meantime, Mindy's graduation dress had gotten snug around the tummy. Munching her roll, she studied the menu. There weren't any prices, and she wasn't sure how she was supposed to pick her entrée without them.

"Excuse me," said Joel, standing up.

54

"Well, should we order something for you?" asked Susie. "Do you want some soup?" She looked more annoyed than concerned.

"Mom – shouldn't you help him?" Mindy asked, as Joel shuffled across the dining room. "I mean, come on." Mindy looked around the table for affirmation. Her mother was clearly enjoying her role as self-appointed hostess. Why would she want to get up, just because her husband had cancer?

"Excuse me," said Lauren. She rose and hurried toward the restroom.

"I guess Lauren is going with him," said Susie. "What a lovely daughter you have, Ron. So helpful. Maybe you should go too, Mindy."

"Okay then," said Mindy. She got up and followed the others, leaving Susie and Ron alone at the table. Dashing down the hall, she could still hear her mother's trilling laughter.

"Dad, are you okay?" Mindy asked. He was listing near the Gents Room door.

"I'm not sure," he said, bracing himself against a wall. "Maybe I should go home."

"I'll go with you," Mindy offered uncertainly. He did look awfully gray, and she didn't want him hurling on the brown flowered carpeting. That would be the icing on her cake of humiliation.

"No, it's your special night, Honey. You stay here. Mom can take me."

"I just want to check on Lauren first."

In the Ladies Room, Lauren drooped miserably on one of a row of floral poofs in front of a mirror that extended the length of the room. Apparently some interior decorator from the ancient past had imagined a line of ladies perched on poofs and powdering their noses. Mindy knelt next to Lauren, who was crying softly.

"I miss my mom," Lauren said.

"You can have mine," offered Mindy. "But be careful what you wish for."

"I know," said Lauren. "But you're just so lucky, and you don't even know it. I didn't have anyone to help me with my dress or my hair. Nobody even cared that I graduated."

Mindy remembered the spat she had with Susie over whether she could go to Hair by Georgio for an updo. Susie didn't want to spend the eighty bucks, and Mindy accused her of failing to recognize the day's importance. But, she had to admit, Susie's mascara did look a little streaky after the ceremony, and not just from sweat.

"I'm so sorry, Lauren," said Mindy. "I'm here for you. I care. Your dad does too."

"Dad," said Lauren. "I don't even want to think about him."

"He seems like he's trying," said Mindy.

"Yeah. So is your mom."

Mindy reached over and gave Lauren a hug. "You're right."

They both stood and left the Ladies. Mindy stopped next to her father, who had collapsed into a stiff chair designed for shrunken but regal old women. "You go on," she said to Lauren. "I'll be there in a minute."

Lauren nodded and continued into the dining room. "You know what, Dad?" Mindy said, "I don't really want to be here, and I've got my own party later." Mindy realized she actually didn't want to be here, and she liked feeling noble too. "Let's let Mom have a nice dinner. I'm sure she'll get home in time for me to go the party."

Mindy left her father slumped in the lounge and returned to the table. "Dad's not feeling good," she announced. "I think I'll take him home."

"Are you sure, Honey?" asked Susie. "Maybe I should go?" she murmured weakly.

"No, Mom, you stay. Your salad's here," Mindy said, as the waiter popped a pear and endive plate in front of her.

"Well, it does look good," said Susie.

"I'll go with you," said Lauren, rising from her chair and setting her napkin on the table. "Maybe I can help."

Ron looked confused. "Maybe I should check on Joel."

"Oh, he'll be fine," said Susie. "This happens all the time. I'm sure he just pushed it today, with all the excitement. The girls probably want to be on their own anyway, talk about the day, rest up before tonight's big event. If you take care of Dad, maybe we can bring you back some dessert. I'm sure they have lovely desserts here."

"We can do that," said Ron. He still looked unsure.

"You girls can take our car, and Ron can drop me home. If that's all right, Ron?"

"Yes, of course," he said.

"Good, then everyone's happy," said Susie, picking up her fork. "Thank you, Girls. We'll see you soon. Mindy, tell your father to go straight to bed."

57

As Mindy turned to leave the dining room, she could hear her mother's lilting voice. "Well, this is nice. Now, Ron, tell me about your work. I've always thought being a lawyer must be fascinating."

Yes, her mother was an idiot, Mindy thought. But she supposed she was lucky to have a mother at all. In a couple of months, Mindy would be at the University of Indiana, and her mother would still be here, emptying basins of vomit. Mindy was doing a mitzvah. Surely she would be rewarded for that.

Chapter Five

Meredith shivered her way through the backyard, peeled off her jacket – in June, ridiculous! -- and wound through the living room to the small foyer of her Wilmette split-level. There, she dropped her briefcase, kicked off her shoes, and scraped up the usual circulars and bills from the floor under the mail slot. Maggie's and Lucy's sneakers and Lucy's pink backpack signalled that her daughters had arrived home from school, and that Maggie was doing her homework upstairs. Retracing her steps, Meredith tossed the mail on the kitchen counter and considered her dinner options. Leftover chicken from last night suggested quesadillas. She also had eggs for omelets, which would play if she made pancakes too. And spaghetti with cheese melted on top was a classic.

These high-carb prospects brought her to the extra five pounds she wore around her waist like an inflatable pool toy, the weight she swore every morning that she would lose, a thought she overrode every night while inhaling an ample bowl of ice cream in front of the TV news. Every day she told herself that if she lost five pounds her life would transform into a romantic adventure, with petty thieves, sleazy defense lawyers, and security guards falling at her feet. Maybe without the five pounds, Alex wouldn't have left her for Shawna. Could that be true, did her husband of ten years dump his family over five pounds of cellulite? It couldn't be that simple. He had seemed pretty attracted to her at this weight just a few months ago. He had seemed to want her back. Now he was gone for a year with Shawna, and she didn't know what that meant. She would make the omelets, but she wouldn't eat the pancakes. Well, maybe just one.

As she broke and whisked the eggs, Meredith thought about her ridiculous day. She had prosecuted a man for stealing CD's, spare change, and a coffee mug from unlocked cars parked on Forest Avenue. She had defeated the First Amendment defense of a New Trier sophomore who had spray-painted, "This place sucks," on the school's brick façade in a fit of picque. She plea-bargained with a homeless man who had entered the Evanston Women's Club at six a.m. and made himself a tuna sandwich. In exchange for his promise not to do it again, Meredith gave him a list of social service agencies and her own lunch. Sometimes she just wanted to cry.

She pulled out the pancake mix and turned on the burners under two large pans. "Lucy, come down and set the table," she yelped, the opening salvo in what promised to be several unrequited cries for help.

Meredith had also closed the Block case today, at least in her own mind. For the Glencoe Public Safety Department, it had barely been a case from the get-go. Falling through a glass table, Marcia Block had met a terrible, violent death. But, despite Lauren's statement that her parents had argued just before she died, Meredith could not find any evidence that Ron had wanted Marcia dead, let alone that he had killed her.

By all accounts, Ron Block was a successful lawyer whose only crimes were workaholism and taking his family for granted. His secretary, potentially a valuable source of information about his extracurricular/extramarital activities, reported that, except for hurling a Lucite cube at the wall and kicking a credenza, Ron was consistently nonviolent, decent and professional. He had never been arrested or investigated for misconduct. According to Lauren, Marcia worried that Ron wanted to have an affair, but Meredith found no evidence that he was doing so. Ron refused to speak with Meredith, which was his right. In his place, Meredith would have done the same.

Did Ron Block get away with murder? It was possible. But Meredith had learned a long time ago that she had to accept the limits of the legal system. Sometimes criminals walked free so that innocent people wouldn't go to jail. She needed real proof to convict someone of murder. She didn't have that here, and she didn't think she ever would, and she accepted that. She couldn't know everything, and she couldn't always dispense justice. That's why people invented God.

"Lucy, come set the table! Now! Maggie, time for dinner!"

Lucy stomped down the stairs and flung three placemats into reasonable position on the dining room table. After throwing three unfolded napkins and three salad forks on top of them, she sat down and waited for service.

"Maggie, would you please pour drinks? Lucy, we need syrup."

"Syrup, yay!" Lucy sprang up, her enthusiasm restored.

"Mags, how was your exam today?" As a seventh grader, Maggie had dipped a toe into the wonderful world of final exams, an unpleasant ritual Meredith did believe was helpful in learning.

"It was okay. Math tomorrow, and then I'm done." Maggie carried two glasses of milk to the table, where Lucy had reseated herself.

Meredith took her plate and Lucy's to the table, and Maggie got her own. Seated head bent in a moment of relief, Meredith contemplated her good fortune. This was her grace, her prayer before her meal. Evaluating the plates of food, she saw that she had provided a reasonably nutritious, basically homemade dinner for herself and her children. The girls were healthy and mostly clean, and their manners weren't too terrible if she ignored Lucy pulling pancakes into pieces with her fingers. Meredith looked at her little world and saw that it was good. And she had created it, she had made everything on this table and around it, with some help and good luck. The only thing missing, the planet that had spun off into an alternate universe, was Alex.

"I can't believe you finish school this week!" Meredith said brightly. "So, next week Extended Enrichment starts. That should be interesting! The bus will pick you up and bring you home, just like usual. In the afternoon…."

"Shawna used to watch us in the afternoon sometimes," reminisced Lucy, twirling her fork in omelet cheese. "We had fun."

"Well, Shawna is in Florida now," said Meredith, who had appreciated Shawna's willingness to help with the girls.

"I don't want to go to Enrichment. Can't we just stay home ourselves?" asked Maggie. "I can take care of Lucy. You could pay me, it could be my summer job."

"Won't you get tired of staying home? I signed you up for this fun ...."

"We just want to stay home," said Lucy. "We can make our own lunch. We know how to do it. We're tired! We just want to rest."

Meredith looked at Maggie. "Are you sure about this?" she asked.

"Yeah, Mom. We'll be fine. Just relax. You worry too much."

"Okay," said Meredith cautiously. "I'm not pulling you out officially yet. But we'll give it a try." Life is changing, she thought, rinsing the dishes and slotting them into the dishwasher. Maggie is almost in eighth grade, and soon she will be in high school. Meredith needed to let them grow up.

After wiping the counter, Meredith sorted the mail. That was when she finally saw the letter, a plain white business envelope, her name scrawled in familiar meticulous longhand. Defying medical protocol, Alex wrote in perfect third-grade teacher script, flat on the bottom and in a straight line, as if his pen were bumping against a ruler. In place of a return address, he had sketched a Mickey Mouse head. Staring at the envelope, she brushed her fingertip lightly over her name, which he had written. Composing herself – it was only a letter, probably about the children or some financial issue -- she ripped it open and unfolded a plain sheet of white paper. He had written each word by hand, in blue ink.

June 1, 1997

Dear Meredith,

We are now getting settled in Orlando. Work is fine, and it's ridiculously hot. I hope you and the girls are doing well.

I know you are probably wondering about this sudden Florida move. After much reflection, I decided that we should spend some time apart. A few months ago, I tried to pull you closer to me. I spent more time with you alone and more time with the kids, our family. I loved it. It was wonderful, and it felt so right. I think you liked it too, but I know I was putting you in an awkward position. I am married. It wasn't fair.

I know I need to resolve things with Shawna. In many ways, I have not been a good husband to her, and that is at least partly because of my attachment to you. I need to give her a chance, and I can't do that when I am always seeing you and the kids. Part of me is hoping that someone will spot her at the pool in her bikini and that will be that. Ha ha, not so funny, I know. Maybe when we are by ourselves, I will be able to see her more clearly, for better or worse. She is young, but I knew that going in. I haven't been fair to her, expecting her to be young and also to be you. I've been very mixed up.

Once you were my wife, and you trusted me, and I threw that away. I wasn't the first idiot in the world, but I was your idiot, and I can't tell you how sorry I am. I know I hurt you deeply, and that I can never make that up. You only deserved my respect and my love. If I didn't know that before, I certainly know it now. I don't know what to say except that I am so sorry, Meredith. I know that's not enough, but it's true.

Partly this is my penance. Because I miss you. You have my phone number for emergencies, but let's just leave it at *that. I will write to you, so you know I'm alive. Otherwise, I need to focus on my work and my marriage. I will call the girls sometimes when you are at work. I miss them so much too, and I want them to know they still have a father who loves them very much.*

Please take good care of yourself. You are very precious. I know that now.

Love,

Alex

Meredith folded the letter and put it back in the envelope. She resisted her lawyerly urge to parse each clause for its specific meaning, because she knew he hadn't written it like that. He was trying to give Shawna a chance. That is what he said. Whether he loved Meredith, whether he wanted to be with her, all of that was irrelevant. He had married Shawna, and that meant something. If he knew that much, maybe he was finally growing up.

Lucy walked into the kitchen. "Mom, what's for dessert? I'm starving."

Meredith wiped her eyes. She grabbed Lucy and hugged her tight. "You really need dessert after pancakes?"

"Pancakes were dinner. Do you have any ice cream? Mom, quit squeezing."

Meredith let go and opened the cupboard. She took out two bowls and the scoop. Tonight she might have ice cream twice. Even after pancakes.

Summer

Chapter Six

July 1997

Tugging her sweater tight in the air-conditioned chemotherapy room of the Kellogg Cancer Center, Susie stared at her husband's ashen face and wished for Frosted Flakes. That's what Kellogg should have done, endowed this place with a lifetime supply of snack packs, instead of fancy I.V. chairs and the live harp music that wafted in from the waiting room like a preview of coming attractions. The walls were a dreary beige, and the TV mounted below a 1980's wallpaper border showed a quivering pattern of high tech snow.

"Sorry, the cable is out today," the receptionist had reported as they checked in.

Neither this news, nor the rows of exhausted, turbaned women drooping on chairs in the waiting room, inspired much cheer. And despite the oncologist's initial optimism about his case, Joel was dishearteningly sick. Susie wondered if the cure were worse than the disease.

"How is he doing?" A small blonde nurse sporting kitten scrubs and a nametag that said "Katie," hurried in to check Joel's I.V. bag. The tubing snaked into a port surgically implanted in his chest, for easy access to his blood supply. He was a vampire's dream, a wine bottle with a screw-on cap. "Looks like maybe an hour more," Katie said. "Has he been sleeping long?"

"I don't know. Sometimes he just rests." With his eyes open like a lizard, she thought. Here, with Susie perched vigilant in a stiff visitor's chair, Joel dozed aggressively, making up for the nights at home in bed when he sweated and squirmed, depriving Susie of a decent sleep. After three hours of shivering and recrossing her legs, Susie wanted to shove Joel to the floor, to grab his blanket and curl up in his lounge chair and close her eyes. She had studied the *People* magazine she brought from home, scanned the "Second Look" feature for differences between two apparently identical photos of Reba McIntyre at the Country Music Awards, and browsed all of Evanston Hospital's helpful pamphlets about how to spot cancers on various body parts. And she was tired, so tired.

"We put something in the I.V. to relax him," said Katie. "I'm sure he needs a good sleep."

"Hey, I'll have what he's having!" said Susie recklessly. "Sorry." She smiled, and her eyes filled with tears.

"Why don't you go to the café and grab some lunch and a cup of hot coffee," said Katie, taking Joel's pulse. "It's just down the hall."

"If you think there's time." After sitting with him faithfully, Susie didn't want Joel to wake up and find her gone.

"Of course there's time. Don't worry, he's not going anywhere for a while." Katie walked out. Okay, fine. If Susie collapsed or lost her marbles, it wouldn't do Joel any good. She walked out of the room, through the waiting area, and into the cathedral-like lobby of the hospital's women's wing, its gift shop displaying carnation arrangements and Mylar balloons for the new mom. Immediately relief flooded her, and she realized how much Joel and his situation were dragging her down. Normally a cheerful person, she felt stressed and demoralized, exhausted and half crazy. She didn't even recognize herself, and she certainly didn't recognize Joel.

After bolting a pizza slice and a paper cup of tepid tea, Susie ran through the hospital's main lobby, its ghostly player piano echoing, keys pressed by some mall musician who had died upstairs. Everything was hard and cold and smelled vaguely of disinfectant. Passing the information desk, she hurried through the automatic door into the blessed summer heat. In the parking circle, an old wife helped her frail husband from a wheelchair into the passenger seat, and a pale young mother buckled her newborn into a car seat while her husband fidgeted. Women took care of everyone, from the cradle to the grave. As soon as that young couple arrived home, the husband was going to park himself in front of the Cubs game while his wife nursed the baby, changed its diapers, and bled profusely into her Kotex pad. And the old guy would want a bath and a hot lunch. Susie was so tired of taking care of people. She was tired of taking care of Joel.

The sun was a gift after the freezing hospital room. Ignoring the pamphlet she had just read about melanoma prevention, she stood on a patch of grass and let sweet, searing rays bedazzle her face and arms and back. How could Joel be so sick in the summer, on such a beautiful day? The trees and flowers were bursting with life and health. She crossed the entrance road to the garden beside the parking garage and sat on a wooden

71

bench. Heat soaked into her bones. It felt like God. She closed her eyes and willed herself to join with nature. Over the sound of leaf blowers, she could just hear a bird chirp. Maybe it was a robin with a new nest of chicklets. Or maybe that was gum. She had no idea what different birds sounded like, which suddenly struck her as sad. Nature was beautiful, and she was part of it, she should be more aware of it.

Her head bobbed, and she jerked upright. She must have slept for a moment, the sun, the pizza. What time was it? Damn, she had been gone for fifty-five minutes. Well, maybe it was forty-five, her watch could be fast. She hurried back into the building and through the refrigerated halls to the Cancer Center.

"Where have you been?"

Splayed out in his chair while Katie unplugged the I.V. from his chest, Joel leaned forward just enough to spit out the accusation with his forked lizard tongue. Spent, he lay back against the head rest, his eyes yellow slits. Having refreshed herself in the outer world, Susie now noticed the yellow cast to Joel's skin, a sour pastel, like lemon juice.

"He's looking a little jaundiced," Katie reported matter-of-factly. "We put in a call to Dr. Gold. We'll see if he wants to do anything."

Grand. Now they would have to sit here until the oncologist had time to call back. The problem with dealing with Dr. Gold was that playing the cancer card did not get him excited. Susie wondered what it was like when eighty percent of the people you dealt with had cancer. If they were as crabby as Joel, you would probably be tempted to let them die. Or worse.

"Joel, how are you feeling?" Susie asked, as Katie breezed out of the room. She hardly cared anymore, but she felt it was her job to inquire.

"Awful," he said, his eyes still slits. "I want to go to the bathroom." With great effort, he leaned forward and swung his legs around to the side of the chair.

"Let me help you." She reached for his arm to steady him.

Joel stood and closed his eyes. "Dizzy," he said. "Just give me a moment." He placed one hand around her waist, and with his other he reached for the wall.

Slowly, they inched their way down the hall. Joel stopped to rest every few steps. He hadn't eaten all day, and his system was coursing with poison. Maybe this was the way rodents felt after eating the pellets that his company, AA Ants Away Pest Control, provided to destroy them. Maybe the universe was run by a giant rat, and this was some kind of poetic justice. Susie pushed the men's room door open and went in with Joel.

"You can't," he protested weakly.

"Give me a break," she said. But, despite all she had seen, she wanted to allow him some illusion of dignity. "You go into the stall," she said. "I'll be right out here if you need me.

Joel leaned his weight on the metal door. It swung in, and he fell forward, pitching into the stall and onto the hard tile floor. His head missed the toilet by inches. "Oh, God," he moaned. He lay on his stomach groaning, his arms and legs scrabbling like a bug flipped on its back.

"Oh, Joel, I'm so sorry," moaned Susie, leaning over him, rubbing his back.

"Where were you?" he said, and this time she didn't know if he were talking to her or to God.

"Let me get help," Susie said, moving toward the door.

"No," Joel said. "Look." He moved to his side. His pants were wet. He started to cry.

"It's all right, Honey." She knelt down on the bathroom floor next to her husband and put her arms around him. "Poor thing. I shouldn't have taken you by myself."

Joel tried to sit up. "It's not your fault," he said slowly, as if understanding this for the first time. "I'm sorry to put you through all this. It's not what you signed up for."

"Of course it is. We promised for better or worse, in sickness and in health. This is the sickness part. Then there will be health. Let me get the nurse."

"No, no nurse. No emergency room, no oncologist, no more. I want to go home. Can you please take me home?"

Susie went into the hall. Near the front door, she found a wheelchair. Without saying anything to anyone, she wheeled it through the waiting room and into the men's room. She figured out how to put on the brake, and together, she and Joel managed to slide him onto the seat. With great authority, she pushed her husband back down the hall and out the front door to their car, parked in the small lot for cancer patients in front of the Center.

"You sure about this?" she asked. "We haven't talked to Dr. Gold."

"Screw Dr. Gold," he said. "I don't think I can do this anymore." Susie helped Joel into the passenger seat. Of course he would keep going with his treatment, but for now he was tired, and he needed a break. The hospital was frustrating and surreal, and he had had enough for today. "Look at all the green leaves," he said, as Susie drove north on Sheridan Road. "And the sky is so blue. I didn't even remember that it's summer. What if I miss the whole thing? And Mindy will go off to college next month. This could be our last time together. I don't want to spend it like this."

Susie glanced over at Joel. The seat belt over his shoulder was keeping him upright, but he listed slightly toward the door. She reached down and hit the lock button.

"Do you want to stop at Gillson Park and look at the lake?" she asked. "I'm sure it's beautiful. We could open the windows."

"No thanks. I just need to get home, change my pants. I'm sorry," he said.

Continuing up Sheridan to Glencoe, Susie glanced at Joel periodically. She had given him an empty paper cup in case he needed to vomit, but he didn't use it. He just sat listless, his yellow-gray skin blending into the tan seat covers. His body had no contrast, no red lips, no hair, as if he were disappearing. She pulled into the garage on Sunset Lane, turned off the car engine, and sat quietly. Beside her, Joel breathed softly.

The garage was custom designed to fit Joel's business. The walls to either side of the door held shelves, rows and rows of shelves, holding pesticides of all kinds. There were aerosol cans of insecticide with names like Invader and Stingray, plastic canisters of ant pellets, and boxes of a product called In Tice sweet ant gel which claimed, "They'll die for the taste," and which was delivered through a syringe, like medicine. Higher shelves, accessed with a folding step ladder, held plastic buckets of rodenticides – Fastrac, Contrac, and Final, strong anticoagulant pellets for rats and mice. The tippy top shelves were for outlawed or out-of-fashion rat poisons containing arsenic. Joel didn't like to advertise his rodent-killing service too openly. Some North Shore residents wanted squirrels, raccoons, chipmunks, and even mice to be dealt with humanely – trapped and released in a distant forest preserve to make their way back to someone else's basement or attic. Others didn't care, or they were freaked out enough that a nest of rodents was living in their walls to want them gone, period.

When Mindy was little, Susie didn't allow Joel to keep his supplies here. Although the danger was minimal, she was afraid of a freak accident, and she wasn't taking chances. Now that Mindy was in high school, Susie permitted it, since Joel preferred it. He said it was more convenient. She looked again at Joel, who seemed to be stirring. A little poison killed cancer cells. A lot of poison – she thought of mice, their veins opening, bleeding to death on the inside, and then of Marcia Block, pumping out her life's blood on the kitchen floor. Stepping out of the car, she heard a noise behind her and jumped.

"Susie. I came by to visit Joel and to thank you for the cookies last week. Can I help you get him into the house?"

Ron Block walked around the car to the passenger side. "Come on, Buddy, you're home," he said, opening the door and unfastening Joel's seatbelt.

"Let's get you inside." Gently, Ron eased him out of the car as Susie opened the back door into the house.

Wrapping his arm tightly around Joel's back, Ron led him through the kitchen and into the living room, where he set Joel, cringing, into his favorite lounge chair. Although Ron's house, with its granite and cherry kitchen, master bedroom suite, and multitude of marble bathrooms, was much larger and more luxurious than the Steinmetz's wood colonial, Ron found himself migrating to Joel and Susie's house with increasing frequency.

The truth was, Marcia's death had thrown him. Normally businesslike and efficient, Ron had begun to wonder what all his hard work and cool formality was for. He had earned the respect of his law firm and his clients, he had a beautiful house and a stash of stock certificates and no financial worries.

But he had no wife. Now, too late, he realized all that she had meant to him, all that he had taken for granted. She had always been there for him, in ways large and small. She shopped and straightened, she washed clothes and made dinner. When he opened the refrigerator, he saw milk and grapes and cheese and bread. If Lauren were sick or needed a ride or a new dress or help with homework, Marcia handled that too.

And perhaps most important, she had listened to him. He hadn't poured his heart out to her, he wasn't sure he had one then, his feelings were buried so deep. But he had told her about his day, and she had listened. He had seen an old friend client, negotiated difficult terms, he had fired a lazy associate, chaired a board meeting. Sometimes he felt annoyed with her for forgetting which matter was which, for not knowing which partner had insulted him or eaten lunch with him or been out sick last week. But now he had no one to tell the minutia of his day, to peck hello, to serve him a warm plate of homemade food.

Lauren was almost always out somewhere, and soon she would go to college. Without Marcia, Ron had no one to care for him. The house echoed emptily around him, and he had begun to question his life. He was working less, he had trouble concentrating. He came home early, and no one cared. And then Susie started showing up.

They were a peach of a pair, him with his dead wife, her with her sick husband. She showed up on his doorstep every week with baked goods or a cooked meal. He thought she bought them all at the store, but it touched him that she came, that she remembered him and made the effort when they hadn't known each other before, and with all that she was facing herself. Maybe she liked getting away from her own house, and she didn't feel guilty for leaving Joel on a mission to help someone else. Still, that was a good quality, wasn't it? He started asking her to stay for a while. She always looked pretty, and she smelled like a cinnamon stick. She walked into the kitchen and filled the tea kettle just as if she lived there, and they would sit for a few minutes at the new kitchen table and talk. At first it was just vapid chat, the girls doing this or that, but soon they started talking about their spouses and even about their fears. Joel was so sick, and soon Mindy would leave, and Susie would have to handle it all on her own. Ron liked Joel, and he could see that Joel needed him. He could reciprocate, he could help Susie too.

78

"Joel, how about we get you changed into something more comfortable. Then you can come back here, or do you want to go to bed?"

"Maybe bed is better," Joel murmured.

As Susie watched from the doorway, Ron lifted Joel out of the chair and helped him into the den, where she had fashioned a makeshift daytime bedroom with a fold-out couch and an old TV on top of a low bookcase. Susie scooted ahead to pull down the covers. Joel sat on the edge of the mattress, and Ron took off his shoes.

"Just like Jesus," Joel joked weakly.

"Your humble servant," said Ron. "Can I get you anything – a drink or something?"

"Make it a double," said Joel, as Susie came in with a clean pair of pants and a cup of hot tea.

"Nice and sweet, just the way you like it," said Susie. "It should warm you up." She turned to Ron. "It's freezing in that hospital. A meat locker. And on such a nice summer day." She tugged open a window and took off her sweater. "That will give you a nice warm breeze," she said to Joel.

"Thanks, Honey. You're an angel of mercy."

"Yeah, I am." She handed him the tea. He took a sip and closed his eyes. She took it from him and set it on the coffee table.

"Well, I'll let you rest. You must be tired," said Ron to Susie as they walked into the kitchen. They could hear Joel scuffling with his clothes, and then the creak of springs as he lay down.

Susie stepped out of her shoes. "I am beat, but I would love some company too," she said.

"Let me warm you up," said Ron.

He went to the stove and turned the tea kettle back on. At home, his was beige, to match the counters, but Susie's was bright red. She pulled two mismatched mugs out of the cupboard and stuck in two tea bags, Raspberry Royale. Stretching to reach the honey, her cotton skirt hiked up a bit in the back. Her bare toes were small and straight, dotted with a pearl of frosted pink polish. After pouring the hot water, she scooped her red curls into an elastic band to reveal the back of her freckled white neck. She was comfortable with him, he thought. They took the tea and a plate of cookies into the living room and sat on the couch next to each other. He should be at Eagles & Fitch, or fighting his way home in Friday traffic. But he wasn't, he was here. He sighed.

"Where's Mindy?" he said.

"Still at work. The counselors stay late on Friday to clean up. Speaking of which – you're home kind of early. Not that I'm complaining." She smiled at him.

"Shabbat, you know." He smiled back. "I meant to visit with Joel. How is he doing?"

A shadow crossed Susie's face. "Not good. They act like this is normal, but he feels awful. I hope it helps him. They're going to do some tests next week. I don't even know what they're looking for. They said he was going to be fine, but you can see him. He's miserable."

"And what about you?" asked Ron, touching her arm. Her skin was soft, white satin with a sprinkle of fairy dust.

She looked in his eyes. "Ditto," she said. She bit her full, pink lower lip. "He's awfully cranky," she said, and she started to laugh.

"Really," he said, grinning at her. She was amazing.

She stood up. "I'm going to get us some more tea, and then I want you to tell me all about your day," she said. "Every bit of it. I think it's fascinating."

Chapter Seven

Meredith sat in the last row of the large meeting room at the Winnetka Community House because she wasn't invited to Tiffany McDonald-Cohn's Bat Mitzvah. She felt less like Maleficent than the ticketless Jew on Rosh Hashanah who is told when he enters the synagogue to give his brother a message, "Okay, you can go in, but don't let me catch you praying." Praying was not Meredith's forte anyway, and she found it especially hard to go spiritual while a tap dancing class reached a frenzied crescendo on the ceiling above her. Apparently this congregation didn't own a synagogue building. Instead, they held services in rented park district rooms, and the rabbi carried the Torah from place to place in the trunk of his car. It was all very desert nomad -- appropriate, Meredith supposed, for American Jews in the diaspora.

With its colonial chandelier and plain plaster walls, this makeshift sanctuary looked like the Paul Revere Conference Room in the Concord Marriott. Consistent with the eighteenth century theme, it had no air conditioning, and the high, angled windows provided only the idea of a breeze. Maggie, legally invited to Tiffany's Bat Mitzvah, sat on the right side of the room with a group of friends. Though they had burst in effervescent in pastel dresses and fruity lip gloss, forty-five minutes of droning amens rising to God in puffs of steam had reduced them to drooping, barely animate dolls. Down the hall, Lucy was leaping around at her friend Ainsley Allen's gymnastics birthday party, where the hostess thoughtfully armed each guest with a Popsicle and a squirt gun.

Although she could have amused herself browsing cool shops in downtown Winnetka for the overlapping hour, Meredith had decided to take the miraculous coincidence of these two life events as a sign that it was time to pay God her respects. Meredith's mother was Jewish, and her father was not. Her childhood had been a hash of latkes and spiral cut ham, with the emphasis on holiday fun, not theology. Sometimes she missed the melancholy Hebrew tunes from the smattering of services she had attended as a girl. At least, this service should provide a moment to sit quietly and feel grateful for the big things – life, nature, the beauty of the world. That seemed better, although damper, than browsing monogrammed stationary.

As a guitar-strumming woman in a bobby-pinned yamulke belted out a Hebrew chant, Tiffany McDonald-Cohn, teetering on heels ostentatiously inappropriate for a newly minted thirteen-year-old, rose from the front row, stood next to the rabbi, and faced the congregation. Seven adults, undoubtedly important Cohns and McDonalds in various phases of sweat-soaked anxiety, stationed themselves behind the rabbi and in front of the ark. Why were there so many? Meredith picked out the four old grandparents and mentally put them in her "identified" box. Grandpa Cohn, muttering the blessing

83

over the Torah, finished with a supportive "amen" from the larger group. Gripping the silver pointer to mark her place in the Torah scroll, Tiffany chanted today's portion in a sweet, shaky soprano that became clearer and stronger as she continued. Singing the ancient tune, she momentarily transformed from a self-conscious junior high kid in sexy shoes to a Jewish angel. Even Maggie and her friends, damply fidgeting on the other side of the room, paused and hushed.

Grandparents finished the blessings and sat, leaving the rabbi, Tiffany, a tall forty-fiveish man, a similar-aged but smaller and chubbier woman in a prim navy suit, and the universal wild card, a much younger, thinner woman with streaky blonde hair and tanned cleavage. Meredith held out slim hope that the odd-woman out was Tiffany's older sister, who had jetted back from her glamorous job as a makeup artist in a Manhattan beauty salon. This attempt at optimism met its usual bloody doom when, during his speech expressing pride in his daughter Tiffany's accomplishment, the man supportively squeezed the blonde woman's shoulders, dangerously plumping her chest. Because of course, this would be an ordeal for the young woman -- perhaps her first public appearance as the wicked stepmother? Tiffany seemed unfazed by the excess of mother figures present on the dais. Her actual mother, inscrutable and hopefully on valium, kissed her daughter briskly.

As the adults resumed their seats, Meredith glimpsed a small bulge in the tummy area of the second wife's pencil skirt. Could a new life be forming there, a miracle from God, the potential for another Bat Mitzvah, this one not attended by Tiffany's mother, in thirteen years or so? Meredith fervently hoped it was just a big bagel. Tiffany pulled a sheet of notebook paper from her prayer book, smoothed it, and cleared her throat. It was time for her Bat Mitzvah speech.

"Today I am an adult. Car keys, Dad?" Tiffany looked at her father, and the crowd chuckled. "But really, that's the point. In the eyes of Judaism, I am a grown woman. I am responsible for my actions. If I do something bad, I must apologize for it and make up for it. I must follow the rules of my religion to the best of my ability. I am supposed to fast on Yom Kippur, and if I make a promise, I must keep it. But in America, I am not an adult. I can't drive or drink or vote or make a contract. I can't get married. So what does this day mean? And does it make any sense?

"As I see it, I am now responsible for my moral behavior. This is even harder than following the law, because moral standards are higher. Nobody is going to put me in jail if I hurt someone's feelings. But if I break a promise, if I make somebody sad, I can't just say, 'Oh, I'm a kid, I didn't know what I was doing.' It will be completely my fault. Because God made people with free will. When we do something wrong, it's not God's fault. It's ours.

"Yet, this is a happy day. The fact that I am a responsible adult is supposed to be a good thing. So, there must be an upside to this. Maybe because sometimes I will do good things. Like today, when we are giving all of our canned vegetable centerpieces to the New Trier Food Pantry. Maybe it's also a happy day because my parents aren't as responsible for me as they once were. I am an adult, and they don't have to look out for me as much. So I want to say, thanks, Mom and Dad, for all you have done for me to bring me to this great day. I know it was a lot."

Tiffany sat down next to her mother and gave her a kiss on the cheek. Her mother reached over and gave her a big hug. The rabbi raised his arms in blessing over Tiffany and her entire family. And the congregation stood to praise God, pray for peace, and remember the dead.

After kicking off her shoes in the foyer, Meredith scooped up the mail and climbed the stairs to the hall bathroom to wash off her sweaty make-up. For her, a good Sabbath meant a clean face, bare feet, and reheated leftovers for lunch. She had dropped Maggie and a couple of friends at the Italian phase of the McDonald-Cohn celebration, an air-conditioned lunch in the basement of Maggiano's restaurant. After a break, the festivities would continue at the Palladium, Glenview's roller rink. Hopefully, they would not conclude as did the last such party, with a morphine nightcap and a cast for the Bar Mitzvah boy in the Evanston Hospital emergency room. In her bedroom across the hall, Lucy, after her morning exercise and pizza lunch, was polishing off the peanut butter cups in her goody bag.

As she brushed her teeth, Meredith spotted a hand-addressed envelope protruding between the electric bill and a circular advertising SAT tutoring. It was another letter from Alex, her second since he had left. Staring at the envelope, she continued brushing. Just because he wanted to communicate didn't mean that she should change her plans. She would get to the letter in her own time.

Meredith thought about the first letter. It was easy to be seduced by its sweetness, by the love that he expressed. But the bottom line was that Alex was staying with Shawna. All the hearts and flowers would only confuse her if she let them, and she couldn't afford that, not for herself, and not for her children. If Alex wanted to keep in touch, that was interesting. But she couldn't let it mean anything. She walked into her bedroom, shut the door, and shakily tore open the envelope.

July 1, 1997

Dear Meredith,

Work is going fine. There are lots of geriatric patients here to help with my research project, and the hospital is well-run and supportive. I will be able to gather a lot of data, and I am determined to do that and not stay a minute more than the year I signed on for. Because the truth is, I miss you too much.

I don't know what I was thinking when I left. I was crazy to let Shawna convince me that she and I needed more time together, and that would change our marriage for the better. I think I felt guilty because of my feelings for you, and because of what I did to you. I didn't want to make the same mistake twice, hurting my wife because I thought I loved someone else. I needed to be sure that I was following my heart and my head, and not - well, some other part of my anatomy, which is fickle and not to be trusted.

Meredith put down the letter and sat on the bed. He was trying to be honest, which was a step in the right direction, but this was too much information. How was she to know that his divining rod wouldn't find water in some other underground cavern if he decided to come back to her? Well, she had lost her appetite anyway. She might as well finish the thing.

Meredith, I miss you. Shawna is fine, but she is not my friend, and time and distance from you will never change that. I knew you were for me from the beginning, from that first date when I was a resident and you let me sleep through "Jaws" and the popcorn clean-up afterwards. You were so kind to me. And I didn't know what I had, or after a while I took it for granted. But now I don't.

I am going to stick it out down here, because I want to do this research, and because I am learning even more about how much I need you and our children in my life. But please know that I miss you. When I left you and the kids, I made the biggest mistake of my life. I know that now.

Okay, Shawna is calling me to leave for dinner, so I have to go. She has made some new friends here in the gated community, from the pool and the tennis courts, I guess. So, we are all going out to dinner at the golf club. There should be a lot of back-slapping, and Shawna can wear some of her new summer clothes. I have to try to be a good sport and get through this year somehow.

Love,

Alex

Meredith put her head in her hands and started to cry.

Chapter Eight

August 1997

Finally, breathed Mindy, sunny side up on a faded towel at Glencoe Beach on an actual nice day. When early June wasn't cold, it was weirdly hot, the sand searing and the water icy to the point of pain, a choice between the frying pan and a swim in a Slushy. By mid-June dead fish started washing up, big silver ones with flat, opaque eyes, in a stinking zigzag along the shore. July brought a plague of biting flies, nipping her ankles until she fled to the parking lot. Mindy couldn't imagine what would happen next, blood or frogs.

But today was perfect, sun on sparkling water, cartoon clouds in a baby blue sky, and the sand warm as an incubator through her towel. Toddlers in tutus and saggy diapers staggered between the lake and their nannies, who chatted in choppy English along the water's edge, while mothers gossiped in squat beach chairs. It was the Garden of Eden, if Eden bordered Lake Michigan and had a snack bar with Super Ropes.

"Where's your sunscreen? You need some goo." Mindy frowned at Lauren's back, her white skin a sinister pink between her bikini top and bottom. Her spine stuck out like a bead bracelet under a tight silk sleeve.

"It's there somewhere. Just browse around." Eyes closed, her cheek on her towel, Lauren waved languidly in her bag's general direction.

"Okay, I've got it," said Mindy, shoving aside tampons, loose change, and melting Lip Smackers. "Hold still." As if that were an issue. Lauren hadn't moved since they arrived at the beach forty-five minutes ago. She just lay inert under the midday sun as if waiting to vaporize. "All done. Okay, turn over now – and sit up. Look, I've got juice boxes, and mini bags of pretzels. You're sweating out all your ions or something."

Lauren turned and propped herself on her elbows. "Electrolytes. You are such a dork. You'll fit right in at Indiana."

Mindy blinked beneath her sunglasses. She and Lauren always teased each other, that was part of being best friends. But lately, Lauren had lost track of the thin but all-important line between an intimate tweak and just plain nasty. Yes, Lauren's mother was dead, and that was tragic. But Mindy's dad was sick, and she still tried to consider other people's feelings. Misery was no excuse to be a jerk.

Lauren sat up and took a juice box from Mindy's towel. Mindy couldn't see Lauren's eyes behind her sunglasses, but she was cooperating, which was as close as she ever came to an apology. "I can't believe you brought these," she said slowly. "My mom always had a purse full of juice boxes and goldfish crackers when I was little. She was like a magician, producing an endless supply of snacks." Lauren tilted her cat face toward Mindy. "I know you're trying to take care of me. But you can't, you know. Be her, I mean."

"I know," said Mindy. "I just don't want you to – vanish in a puff of smoke." Feeling fat next to Lauren – well, who wouldn't, in her size zero bikini she was right on the border between chic and gross – Mindy sucked in her stomach beneath its panel of black lycra. Lauren leaned back on one hand, took a dainty sip of apple juice, and nestled the box in the sand. "You shouldn't look down your nose at Indiana, you know," said Mindy. "Lots of kids from New Trier go there. And look at you. You worked your butt off, and you didn't get into your reach school. I mean, I'm sure Skidmore will be great, but it's not what you were shooting for."

"Yeah, I know. I see it every time my father tells somebody where I'm going. He kind of spits it out. My mother wrinkled her nose when she said it, like she was smelling skunk."

"Your mom didn't seem like that – snobby, I mean," said Mindy. "Where did she go to college, anyway?"

"Indiana." Lauren smiled, and then frowned. "But sometimes those parents are the worst. I don't know what they think is so special about Ivy League schools. They probably don't think about it at all, about what the actual experience will be like. It's just a cool sticker for their car window and something to brag about at cocktail parties. They keep leaning on us, pushing us to work harder, when they probably spent their high school careers chugging beer and mooning each other. And then, when we don't get in, because it's all a crap shoot anyway, or colleges getting paid off, then they're so disappointed in you. They make you feel like garbage."

Lauren's hands were shaking. With a tight fist she smashed her juice box and started burying it in the sand. Mindy reached over and touched her arm. "But you did so well at New Trier, you were amazing. All those A.P.'s. It's not your fault. It's ridiculous."

"It's like I was just this grade-making machine. They didn't care if I learned anything, just if I got enough points. And you know, I could have handled that, if they didn't act so disgusted when I didn't get in. When it came down to the choice I actually had, I think my parents wanted me to go to Skidmore because it sounds fancy. I don't think they even cared how I would like it, and they certainly didn't care what kind of education I would get. Even in April, after I got all my acceptances and rejections and it was totally over, they were still obsessing about it. Maybe if they had hired a different tutor for my application essay, maybe if I had dug latrines in Peru, maybe if they had made me stay home and work on Friday nights, maybe then I would have gotten into Harvard and their lives would have been god damned perfect." She grabbed a sharp stick and jabbed it into the burial mound, where it drained the juice box dry.

Seagulls floated on the water and dove for fish. Mindy took a pretzel. "It's so weird that we're actually going away in like, two weeks. Do you ever think about staying – like, for your dad?"

"You mean because he'll miss me so much? Forget it. He's a robot. He doesn't care about me."

"I don't know. It seems like he's trying, like he's around more. I never used to see him when I would come over, and now he's there sometimes. He comes to our house too every once in a while, to visit my dad." Mindy bowed her head. "Maybe he's gotten better, after all this."

"He seems sad sometimes. So maybe there's a heart in there somewhere." Lauren paused. "How is your dad doing, anyway?"

Mindy took off her sunglasses. "He is so sick. I don't get it. I don't know which is worse, the disease or the cure. I mean, he seemed fine, and then they started poisoning him with all this chemo stuff. He has sores in his mouth, and he can't eat, he throws up all the time, and he's so tired. When he has energy, he worries about his business, especially with me starting college. He's trying to teach my mom so she can help him, which is a joke. It gives her something else to think about anyway."

"What does the doctor say?"

"I'm not sure. I don't know if Mom tells me everything. She definitely wants me to go to Indiana, but I don't know. I'm worried about college, and I'm worried about them. Maybe I should just wait." Mindy stuck her sunglasses back on and started twirling a sprig of her hair.

"No, you've got to go. It's not like you'll be that far away, you can come back if they need you for something. And what can you do anyway? Your mom will take care of your dad. And I'm sure it's no fun over there. Wouldn't it be great to just get out?" Lauren leaned back on her hands and arched her ribs toward the sun.

"I know. But he is really sick."

"I'm sure he wants you to go."

Mindy looked at Lauren quizzically. For someone who didn't know her dad or anything about cancer, she had a lot of opinions. The sky began to darken, and the breeze began to gust, picking up sand and the edges of their towels. Mindy put her foot on the empty pretzel bag. She felt a sprinkle of rain.

"Maybe we should leave," she said.

"Yeah." Lauren stretched her arms. "I really am sorry about your dad. I bet he'll get better. But even if he doesn't, at least you can kind of understand it. It's sort of nature taking its course. Not like my mom. Who would think that falling off a ladder in the kitchen would kill somebody? It doesn't make sense. And it's such a shock. At least you can talk to your dad, tell him you love him. I never had the chance with my mom. She was warning me not to step on glass, and then she was dead. Even at the end she was trying to micromanage me."

Mindy stared at Lauren. "She was trying to protect you. She was being a good mom."

"I know," said Lauren. "Bad joke. She was a good mom, most of the time. A really good mom."

Lauren and Mindy shook out their towels. The rain was getting heavier, and the sky was almost black. As they picked up their sandals and beach bags, an announcement came over the loudspeaker.

"Due to the threat of lightening, we are closing the beach. Please clear the area."

Lauren and Mindy followed the crowd up the ramp to the parking lot, where they found Susie, anxiously staring out her car window. "Mom, what are you doing here?" said Mindy. "We can just walk to Lauren's. It's not a big deal."

"When you're at college, I won't know what you're doing, and that's fine. But while you're still here, I'm going to make sure you're safe."

"Ow!" Lauren said. Pellets started falling from the sky and bouncing off the hood of the car. Hail. Mindy and Lauren opened the car doors and hurled themselves inside.

"See?" said Susie. "Sometimes I know what I'm doing."

"Thanks," said Lauren from the back seat, as ice pellets pounded the car. "Really. Thanks a lot."

August 6, 1997

Dear Meredith,

It's been rainy here, and so hot. Fortunately, I spend most of my time sealed in the hospital. There aren't even any windows in the lab. I could be anywhere, in a science station in Antarctica, for all I know. It feels like that, being away from you and the kids.

97

Or like I'm in prison, just waiting for my time to be up.

Shawna is trying hard, and sometimes I try too, but I'm just going through the motions. It doesn't matter to me. I keep thinking about you, how smart and pretty and fun you are. All our time together, it meant something. We loved each other, we shared our children. You made a home for us, a real home. I wasn't there enough, and I didn't appreciate you, all you did to make a real, loving home. Somehow I missed it, I took it for granted. I was thinking only about myself.

After I finish this letter, I'll go home here. The air is oppressive, it's heavy and wet and suffocating. You can't even walk outside, not for long, and if you exercise, you'll pass out. The bugs are huge, and everything gets covered with slime and fungus and bacteria. Honestly, people shouldn't live here, not this time of year, anyway. What kind of summer is it when you can't go outside? Everything feels wrong.

Sorry to be such a downer. I miss you, and I love you. This is when we used to go on vacation together, a few weeks before school starts. I remember our trips to Toronto and St. Louis and the Dells. Give the girls a kiss from me, and keep a big one for yourself.

Love,

Alex

Fall

Chapter Nine

September 1997

"Oh, God, Mindy, is that my phone? I don't know what to do with the damn thing! It's got to be your dad!" Susie rummaged in her purse, yanked out the vibrating hot potato, and started pushing buttons. "How do I talk in this thing?"

"Give me that." Mindy snatched it out of her mother's hand. "Hello? You'll have to speak up. We're at the football game, and Kentucky has the ball. Okay, just a sec. It's almost halftime, the marching band is lining up. Yup, plumes on their hats and everything."

Early that morning, Susie had driven to the University of Indiana for Freshman Family Weekend. Joel wanted to come, but he was way too sick. He was always throwing up these days, and anemic – he looked like a vampire in a vegetable patch. Sometimes Dr. Gold stopped chemo to build up his strength, but he put him right back as soon as he thought Joel could stand it. But he couldn't, he couldn't keep anything down, he lived an unending cycle of vomiting and kvetching and sleeping. Of course Susie felt sorry for him, but she was at the end of her tether. Once upon a time last year, she had dreaded the loneliness and emptiness when Mindy went to college. She had worried that rifling through the sale rack at Marshall Fields and vacuuming might not be enough. But with swabbing Joel's face and concocting bland meals he couldn't keep down and answering phone calls for AA Pest Control, she was swamped, her nerves frayed. At night she just wanted to lie in the bathtub with a bottle of wine. Instead, she held Joel's clammy hand and listened to him moan. It was enough to drive even a saint nuts, and Susie was no saint.

So, when, after a particularly repulsive day, Joel had muttered that maybe she would like to attend Freshman Family Weekend alone, Susie had promptly agreed. At great personal sacrifice, considering the length of the drive and her self-diagnosed but very real case of Caregiver Burnout, Susie promised to be gone only one night. She divided a Jewel roast chicken onto three plates for his meals, with large scoops of his favorite instant mashed potatoes and some well-cooked cauliflower. If all else failed, she said, he should eat the mashed potatoes, just to keep up his strength. She left his pills in labeled saucers in the kitchen, along with emergency phone numbers – Dr. Gold, Mindy's dorm room, the Bloomington Hampton Inn. Ron – oh, Ron, just thinking of his strong and generous smile made her weak with gratitude -- had even loaned her his cell phone. She wrote the number on the back of an envelope in bright red Sharpie and stuck it to the fridge with a Hoosiers magnet. Susie had arrived at Indiana only two hours ago, and Joel was already calling. She should have known he would call her for every little thing.

Tooting away, the band strutted onto the field and formed the letter "I." Not that amazing, Susie thought, and she was freezing. Still, no one was barfing on her, at least not yet, she thought, squinting at the overly enthusiastic alums behind her. Mindy was still chatting.

Susie poked her. "What's going on, what's he saying?"

Mindy shook her head. "Yeah, LAUREN," she enunciated, rolling her eyes and pointing to the phone, "it is super great having my mom here. I will be way sad tomorrow when she leaves and I have to go back to drinking beer and hanging out with my friends. Yes, sorry, I know. I am lucky. Yeah. Sorry. Okay, settle down, I said I'm sorry! Talk to you later." She pushed a button and turned to Susie. "That was Lauren. She called to ask her dad for money. She says hello." Mindy gave the phone back to Susie, who eyed it suspiciously. "Mom, it's not a bomb."

"It's just weird, that's all," she said. "I wasn't thinking about Dad before, but now I don't know if it's worse if he calls or if he doesn't."

"If you're worried, call him," said Mindy.

"No way." She stuck the phone back in her purse. "I'm here to see you, at your new school. I am kind of cold, though. How would you feel about leaving? Maybe we could get a snack or something."

"That sounds good," said Mindy, leaping to her feet. She had never been a football fan. "What would you like? After all, this is your crazy twenty-four hours away from Dad. We should do something awesome. There is this great doughnut place...."

Susie glanced smugly at her cinched leather jacket and slim fit jeans. "Perfect -- grease and caffeine

103

are just what I need. And after that, you can show me where your classes are. I want to be able to picture you in your natural habitat. I can't believe you're in college! My little girl, all grown up."

They walked out of the stadium arm in arm, like a greeting card mother-daughter duo. The day was sunny and crisp, a refreshing nip in the air, just chilly if you kept moving. The leaves on the trees were tipped with yellow or bleeding red. Susie felt the glory of fall and also its sadness. Nature burst into its brightest colors and then died. Soon it would be winter, gray and white and bleak. But for Mindy, life was just beginning. She had a new school, new friends, freedom. Today, Susie could almost feel that way herself, that life was exciting, bursting with possibilities. And it was, too – she was young, well, not that old, and she looked very coed in her snug pullover sweater. She would survive this rough patch with Joel and then, who knows? Joel had a terrible attitude, but she was an optimist, like Ron -- look how he had bounced back after Marcia crashed through the breakfast table. Her life would turn around, that's what Ron said. She just had to be patient.

Susie pulled into the garage and goose-stepped out of the car. She had driven four and a half hours with only one stretch break, at an interstate Wendy's where she bought a Diet Coke. The visit had been fun. Mindy was surprisingly not nasty to her, now that she had moved away from The House of Cancer and that the going-to-college experience was turning out fine. Last night they had relaxed over Emperor's Chicken at a

Chinese restaurant, just the two of them. It all brought Susie back to her college days -- the sticky floor, the cheap corrosive wine, and the testosterone-fueled glances from the jocks at the next table in full Indiana regalia. Mindy had confided her fears about her calculus class (too tough), frat boys (too boozy), and her father (too sick). And when Susie responded with advice, Mindy seemed to listen.

"You have a good head on your shoulders, and you can accomplish whatever you set your mind to. If you need help with math, go to office hours and get it. Lord knows, we're paying enough. And wait for a nice, respectful young man – maybe a cute one with a little money, you deserve it. And as for Dad – don't worry, I will take care of him. You just get yourself settled in school here, that is your job right now." Delivering hard-won maternal wisdom, Susie felt good about herself, competent and respected. They kissed goodbye through the car window, and Mindy waved until she was as small as a newborn and Susie's eyes filled with tears.

Now Susie was here in Glencoe, back to reality. The football game, her fortune cookie – "An Attractive Visitor Will Bring Joy to Your Home" – the blessed peace of her bed at the Hampton Inn, they hung around her like an aura. Reaching into the back seat, she tugged out her overnight bag. She felt like she had been gone for ages, even though it was just one night. Nobody could blame her for leaving, she had so needed this break. And Joel had managed, he hadn't even called her once.

Opening the back door, Susie stepped into the kitchen and set her bag and purse on the counter. "Joel, I'm home," she called.

He was awfully quiet. She peeked into the empty den and went into the powder room to pee, a huge relief after all that soda. Back in the kitchen, she expected to see a sink full of dirty dishes. Instead, she found one forlorn plate, gummy with old chicken, potato residue, and mushy cauliflower florets. At least he had eaten his mashed potatoes. But from the look of things, he hadn't eaten anything today, and it was almost 4:00 p.m. Unless Ron dropped by and took him out. He had said he would stop in while she was gone. Maybe Ron took him for brunch at the Club today, that was probably it.

Grabbing her bag, Susie crossed the living room and tip-toed upstairs. If Joel were sleeping, she would leave it in the bedroom and unpack later. But the bed was empty and unmade, its blankets rumpled from a restless night. It must be nice to have a maid, she thought, smoothing the bottom sheet and fluffing the pillows. Everything felt humid and smelled sour. What if Ron came in and helped Joel upstairs? The outing was sure to have exhausted him, it could easily happen. She pulled back the blankets, stripped the sheets, and then jammed them and her dirty underwear down the laundry chute.

She was a bit of a mess herself, she thought, examining her lipstick in the bureau mirror. Clutching her cosmetics bag, Susie walked down the hall to the bathroom. The Steinmetz house had no master bath, and the bathroom that it did have was faded and cramped, the hot and cold water dribbling from two separate faucets. Susie hoped that Ron would never see that.

Oddly, the door was closed. Susie knocked. "Joel, are you in there? It's me, I'm home."

No one answered. Listening, she could hear water, a thin stream leaking out of the faucet and, hopefully, into the sink. Praying that Joel hadn't forgotten and left the water running into a stuffed old drain that couldn't keep up, that water wasn't flowing over the sides of the sink and pooling on the tile floor, Susie turned the doorknob and pushed. She expected to see some watery nightmare, bathroom-turned-aquarium. But it was worse than that.

The door wouldn't open. That wasn't quite true, it opened a couple of inches, but then it stuck on something, and it wouldn't move any more. She pushed harder, and then with all her force. Still nothing. Something was jammed against the door. Stomach churning, Susie went back to the bedroom, picked up the phone, and dialed 911, Glencoe Public Safety.

Chapter Ten

Mindy didn't know if this was a funeral or what. It seemed like less, because it wasn't at the temple or the funeral home, but maybe it was more, because her mother was so completely wrecked that she couldn't plan anything. Apparently her mother had managed to contact a funeral home, because the shoebox on the buffet in the dining room, with a vase of lilies on one side and an old photo on the other, supposedly contained her father. The request for cremation and the call to Mindy had exhausted Susie's strength. Mr. Block had phoned AA Pest Control, Mindy had phoned a few friends, her father's sister, and her grandparents in Pompano Beach – Susie's parents only, her father's parents were already dead – and that was about it. There wasn't a rabbi – Joel and Susie had dropped out of Am Shalom after Mindy's Bat Mitzvah, and Susie didn't want to ask some strange rabbi to speak about a random dead Jew he had never met. As a result, a meager crew, not even a minyan -- Aunt Debbie, a few exterminators, and Mr. Block -- sat in the living room stiffly nibbling the odd assortment of food they had brought. Headachy and nauseous, Susie lay inert in her darkened bedroom at the top of the stairs.

Now in its third day, her migraine showed no sign of letting up.

"Well," said Aunt Debbie brightly. "Maybe we should go around the room and say a few words about Joel. A nice memory of him, something like that."

The exterminators shifted uncomfortably. Mindy, positioned by the doorway in case someone else arrived, backed up a step. She hadn't been to many funerals, but she thought they ought to be in a neutral room, not in her own house. And really, shouldn't there at least be a rabbi? She wasn't sure why, but she thought there should be a rabbi. Her father didn't need one to get into heaven, or wherever dead Jews went, but at least he could give some shape to this thing. They definitely needed a master of ceremonies.

"Okay, well, I'll start," said Aunt Debbie. "Wait, Mindy, ask your mother if she would like to come down. She might like to hear some of this. I'm going to talk about our childhood."

"Fine," said Mindy. "But I don't think she's coming."

Mindy climbed the stairs to her mother's bedroom, formerly the master bedroom. Maybe "master" was just a term of art, a technical real estate word for the biggest bedroom in the house. In which case, this was still the master bedroom. But if it needed an actual master, this room had morphed into something else.

"Mom, can I come in?"

After knocking gently, Mindy turned the knob to see a spongy white lump topped with a frizz of red hair. "Mom, how are you? Aunt Debbie wants you to come down. The – whatever – is about to start. She says you should come down."

The lump rolled, and Susie's head and neck emerged. "I don't feel well."

Damn it, Mindy didn't feel well either. Her father was dead, all she had eaten today was a piece of noodle kugel, a macaroon, and a cherry tomato, and it looked like she was fated to become some Victorian old maid taking care of her mother for the rest of her life. Damn it, she was the injured party here. Her parents had liked each other okay, but she and her dad, they were close. He had talked to her – well, not since she had left for college, he felt like crap, and he had never liked talking on the phone anyway. But she would never have another father, you only got one, and he had really loved her, she knew he had, even if he never exactly said so. Damn it, Susie should be taking care of her, it was her god damn job.

Mindy grabbed hold of the comforter and gave it a good, hard tug. "What are you doing? I'm cold," Susie sniffed.

Susie did look terrible. Her eyes were puffy, and her cheeks were flushed. She chewed on her chapped lower lip and clawed at the covers with a goose-bumpy hand. She looked like the Pillsbury Dough Boy, if he were a hundred years old and run over by a Keebler truck. Mindy sat down and touched her mother's shoulder.

"Mom, they're going to talk about Dad now, say some nice things about him. It'll be good, you can come down and listen. It's for him, Mom, but it's also for you, to help you remember him."

"I remember him," said Susie. "I don't need Aunt Debbie to tell me what he was like. It'll be – annoying. She'll probably tell that story about how he punched out her prom date. The whole point is to prove that once she was hot. I hate that story."

"She probably will, Mom. I hate it too." Mindy started to laugh. It wasn't clean, happy laughter. It was the kind where you're feeling tense, and you know you shouldn't laugh, but it just keeps coming out of you, unsmotherable, until you are embarrassed or cry.

"Why does everything always have to be about her, even her brother's funeral?" Susie grumbled, but she sat up in bed.

"I don't know, but it does. How long do you think it'll take for her to get to that? Like five minutes?"

"Oh, god, I hope not, I hope she doesn't talk that long."

"Don't leave me alone with these people, Mom."

"Who's there, anyway?" Susie swung her legs out of the covers and put her feet on the floor

"I don't know. A few pest control guys, that Audrey from the front desk, and Mr. Block."

Mindy could glimpse life returning to her mother. Her color was better. She touched her hair and stood up. "I just need to freshen up a minute. You go down and tell them I'll be right there."

Susie shuffled down the hall to the bathroom and pushed open the door. The old black and white tile had its usual dull-but-clean sheen, and someone had thrown out the rug. The blood on the edge of the sink, where Joel had hit his head, was scoured off the white porcelain. Only a spindly shadow indicated the shape of the impact and the splash. The overhead fan had done a decent job eliminating the stench of vomit and excrement, and someone, probably Debbie – unless Glencoe Public Safety was completely full service – had saturated the air with the overwhelming odor of fake fruit salad. Susie didn't need Debbie to remind her of Joel, or to present some sanitized version of him. She would never forget him, and especially not her last view of him, bloody and stinking and folded on the floor, after the paramedics had shoved him enough to get the door open to rescue him. Rescue, no, it had been too late – it was a recovery mission, that was all. Susie had told them about the cancer and the chemo and her brief trip to Bloomington, and Dr. Gold, Joel's oncologist, had kindly stopped by to certify the cause of death. The chemo had just been too much for him. Dr. Gold had tried to balance the dose against the persistence of the cancer, but it was not a perfect science. Chemo is poison, everyone knew that. Joel had been poisoned repeatedly, and now he was dead.

The smell in the room, and his ghost, they were enough to make her gag. But she had to be strong, she had to get through this. Her daughter was downstairs, and Ron Block. Susie squeezed a long worm of toothpaste onto her toothbrush and began to scrub.

"Here she is." Ron rose to his feet as Susie stepped off the bottom stair. Her eyes glittered, and her red hair stuck out of her stubby ponytail like sparks. Washed clean by soap and water and tears, her face looked young and open. He walked toward her, took her small, damp hand, and led her to a seat on the couch next to him. He could feel her weight and her softness, as she drooped between him and Phil, the Pest Control assistant manager.

"Good, Susie, you don't look so bad," noted Debbie, sitting primly on the edge of a striped wingback chair. "Would you like something to eat, a glass of wine? Ron brought a quiche."

"Oh." Susie smiled up at him weakly. "Thank you. Maybe later."

"Okay, then," said Debbie. "First, I wanted to tell you all a story about when Joel and I were kids. I am younger than he is, of course, he is the big brother, and he always had to protect me."

Ron stopped listening. He could see Debbie moving, her eyes large and dramatic, her chubby ringed hands brushing her streaked hair away from her face. She was small like Joel, with a dainty nose, but he had been waifishly thin, while she was, well, fat. Well, Joel had been sick the entire time that Ron knew him. They never had a normal guy friendship, if there were such a thing.

Honestly, Ron hadn't had a real friend since high school. He only had business friends, the kind who invited you to the opera gala because they bought a table and then asked you to help their nephew get a job. His relationship with Joel was different. Joel was a nice, ordinary guy who had been dealt a crappy hand. Before Marcia's death, Ron wouldn't have had time for Joel. But now Ron knew what it was like to have something terrible happen out of the blue, something you hadn't planned and didn't deserve. Ron had never done any pro bono work, he had never really helped anyone except by writing checks. But when he met Joel and Susie, he had seen a place to do some good. Ron remembered a rabbi saying that if you save one life, you save the world. Well, he hadn't saved Joel's life, not by a long shot.

Ron heard a soft snort and felt the tickle of her hair as Susie's head nuzzled into his shoulder. "Ahem," said Debbie, looking pointedly at her sister-in-law. "Susie," she said sharply. "I'm about to talk about my wedding."

"Um, I think we need to get back to the office," said Audrey. "Joel would have wanted us to keep the business going. Fall – ant season, they all start coming in the house, so many calls," she said apologetically, as the exterminators stood and stretched.

"Yup. Thanks," said Phil. He turned to Mindy. "So sorry for your loss, Mindy, Debbie. Nice to meet you," he nodded to Ron.

"Please tell Susie to call me if there is anything we can do," Audrey said to the air. They hurried to the front door and left.

"Well, I guess that's it," said Debbie, grimacing.

"Aunt Debbie, I'm glad you're here," said Mindy suddenly. She reached over and squeezed her arm. "I hope you'll stay a while. I have to go back to school tomorrow. I don't want to get too far behind."

"Well, I can stay maybe another day or two, but I have my own life, you know," said Debbie. "Susie is just going to have to get it together. Doesn't she have any friends around here?"

"I'm her friend, I'll help her," said Ron.

"Great," said Debbie, standing up. "I'll clean up in the kitchen."

"I'll help you," said Mindy.

Ron sat on the couch with Susie. Her head had migrated to his chest, and a greasy pink stain rimmed his shirt button where her lipstick had brushed it. No one knew better than Ron what Susie was going through. Marcia had died abruptly, and Joel had been sick for months – they weren't identical situations, but close enough. We all know that our loved ones will die, but when it happens it is an unspeakable shock. And all too soon, the world expects us to continue our lives, to dust ourselves off and move on. Last month, Ron had his work and Lauren and Joel and Susie. Now Lauren was at Skidmore, and the house was so empty. And Joel was dead. Leaving Susie.

"Is everybody gone?" she asked, looking up at him as she moved her head off his chest and rested back against the couch. "Sorry."

"No need to be sorry," said Ron. "You should eat something. I'll go ask Debbie if she knows how to warm up the quiche."

"I don't know why you always wait to find a book until the last minute, Lucy," Meredith scolded. "I doubt there'll be any biographies of famous woman scientists left, especially short ones." She couldn't even think of any besides Madame Curie, and that was ages ago. Oh, yeah, Elizabeth Blackwell, first woman doctor. Did Florence Nightingale count? "You know there are a lot of other kids at Highcrest. Are you the only class doing this now?"

Lucy shrugged and sulked through the automatic door into the Wilmette Public Library. "Miss Damon

115

said that we could do something else if the scientists ran out. I think presidents or actresses or something."

Maggie pushed ahead, past the checkout counter and the slotted bins for returning books and into the fiction section. Meredith turned into the children's room, where she knew that Lucy would pick a book for minimum spine size and maximum illustrations, if there were even a choice to make after all the well-organized Type A fifth graders and their moms had plundered the biography section. Well, let her flounder for a while, thought Meredith, plopping onto the window seat. Maybe that would teach her to start earlier next time.

Meredith sighed and deposited her jacket next to a germy doll house and some well-chewed board books. At 8:30 p.m., a half hour before closing time, the toddler area was empty. Lucy knelt before the biographies, two rows of faded books under a heating vent. A better mother would point her toward the junior high section, to challenge her, but what was the use? Lucy liked TV, shopping, and doing the splits. She was doomed to a humiliating life as a Luvabull or a wife-and-mom. Meredith hoped Lucy would do a better job at the latter than she did.

A small stack of books next to her, Lucy now appeared to be browsing, probably calculating the number of seconds it would take her to read the first sentence of every paragraph and declare victory. Reaching into her purse, Meredith rifled past ripped Kleenexes and gum wrappers to find a white business envelope that promised to be anything but business. Alex's return address, Coconut Cove, sounded like a stop near the peanut brittle cottage on the path to Candy Land. Alex had touched this envelope, he had pushed the letter into its open slot, he had licked the flap. Alright, that sounded like porn. It was just a letter from Alex, probably about his research and his daughters. Flushing, she slid her finger under the flap and removed a plain white page sewn with careful rows of black ink.

September 30, 1997

Dear Meredith,

It's still so hot here, though sealed into the lab as I so often am, I hardly notice it. My research is going well. As you might imagine, there are plenty of elderly patients willing to spend a little of their free time helping expand the horizons of science. Very nice of them, too.

How are the girls?

Meredith paused. She had been right, of course. She could imagine Alex, embarrassed about his earlier letters, now peddling backwards in hopes that a few banalities would wipe his slate clean. He was probably sitting by the pool with Shawna, upside down and slathered with baby oil, her teeny bikini top unhitched to provide an even tan. Yes, he would have explained to Shawna, he was writing to his ex-wife just to assure her that he still cared about their progeny. He did think about them every now and then, between trips to the centrifuge and slathering Shawna with goo.

I really miss them, but not as much as I miss you. Maybe that makes me a bad father, but you are my soul mate. When I am with you, everything feels right, I know that I am home, where I belong. I feel that so much now, with you so far away.

I have tried with Shawna, I really have. I owed her that. But it isn't working, we are just too different. This place, Orlando, it truly is Fantasyland, it isn't real to me. I should be raking leaves and carving pumpkins, not sweating in a golf shirt over a shrimp dinner at the eighteenth hole.

I am going to stick it out here, I am determined, but it is tough. I do have a request for you, and I know I am asking a lot. Are you still willing to send Maggie and Lucy to me for Thanksgiving? I think they would have fun, and I do really miss them. I know that leaves you at loose ends for the holiday, but I don't think Shawna would like it if I asked you to join us. I still need to be respectful of her wishes and to make her as happy as I can under the circumstances.

I will call you soon to see what you think. I hope this will work out for you, I know it is a sacrifice. But it is an excuse for us to talk, even if it is only about travel arrangements. I miss hearing your voice and your funny laugh.

Please take wonderful care of yourself. You are my sweetheart.

Love,

Alex

"Mom, can we get out of here?" asked Lucy. "I'm bored."

Meredith looked up. Lucy was holding the world's thinnest biography. She displayed the cover like a showcase model from "The Price Is Right." "Joan of Arc?"

"Yup," said Lucy. "She got roasted, so it's pretty short. Want to see a picture of her? There are lots."

"Later," said Meredith. She had successfully completed fifth grade. This was not her problem. "Let's find Maggie. Hey, how would you feel about going to your dad's for Thanksgiving?"

"Yes!" shouted Lucy, pumping her arm in triumph. "Last one in is a turkey!"

Sighing, Meredith placed her hand on Lucy's frolicking shoulder. She had been wrong about Alex's letter. He was almost romantic. Could it just be a case of absence making the heart grow fonder? And what was so funny about her laugh? Walking out of the library with her daughters, Meredith knew that this situation would end as they usually did -- with her taking a Cornish hen for the team.

Chapter Eleven

November 1997

Ding! Meredith leaped into the aisle to yank down jackets out of the overhead bin, as Maggie and Lucy reached under their seats to grab M & M's, Mad Libs, and colored pencils and jam them into their backpacks. Although thankfully long past the stage of bouncing Lucy while cramming Maggie full of Cheerios, Meredith's head still throbbed from the stress of travel, the fermenting cabin air, and the tot behind her whose streaming nose and wailing suggested a brewing ear infection.

Not for the first time, Meredith wondered why she was here. She had no desire to go to the Magic Kingdom, and her daughters, who did, were sufficiently competent to manage this journey without her. They had eaten the peanut butter sandwiches Meredith had packed and giggled together over games of hangman, just as they would have if she were back in Wilmette eating pie in front of the TV. And Shawna would meet them at the gate. But Meredith had not been able to shake the image of her daughters, alone and confused, wandering the Orlando terminal, or of oxygen masks falling as they crouched in crash position, crying for their mother. The fact that, if the worst happened and Meredith were on the plane, she would be screaming louder than anyone else, mattered not at all. She could not turn off the mommy gene. Not yet.

So, here she was, enduring fussy babies, a giant credit card bill, and Thanksgiving with her own mother, in order to escort her competent daughters ten feet from the jetway to Shawna. Now Meredith would have to observe her children's betrayal, their delight at seeing their stepmother – slim, tanned, and radically cool – whisk them off in her convertible to activities so awesome that Meredith could not even imagine them. Then Meredith would wait at the Thrifty counter for a Ford compact and drive down a highway peppered with cheesy strip malls and interminable traffic lights to the retirement home, where she would sleep on the fold-out couch in her mother's living room. She should have spent the money to have her head examined.

"Mom, why is the air so thick?" Lucy whined halfway down the jetway.

"It's nice and warm," countered Meredith. "You'll get used to it. That's one of the good things about Florida. It doesn't feel anything like fall does at home."

"Yeah," said Maggie. "Toasty hot. We can swim and eat pumpkin pie on the same day. Cool!"

Cool, thought Meredith. And after Thanksgiving, you can hang popcorn on your palm tree and call it Christmas. They stepped from the heat into the subzero air conditioning of the terminal. Did this place even have real weather? Meredith stopped to pull on her winter coat and then looked up to search for Shawna. But Shawna wasn't there. It was Alex.

Lucy ran up and threw her arms around his waist. Maggie sauntered toward him and then stopped a couple of feet away.

"I didn't expect to see you," said Meredith, playing for time.

He looked wonderful. Despite reported long hours spent staring at Petri dishes in frigid labs, Alex's face and arms were tanned a warm, caramel brown. His graying hair was playfully tussled, and his biceps, under a navy golf shirt, protruded manfully. Hugging Lucy, Alex beamed at Meredith. This fit, handsome, brilliant man, with whom she had created these two lovely girls, was delighted to see her. He reached toward her. She stopped and stood next to Maggie.

"Don't you have to work, Dad? Where's Shawna?" Maggie asked.

"I took the week off," he said. "I wasn't going to miss a minute of your visit."

"Okay," said Maggie cautiously.

"It's nice to see you, Alex," said Meredith. "You look good."

"Same to you," he answered, smiling. He reached up to touch the sleeve of her coat, and she tugged it around her like chain mail. Thank god she was wearing it. If he had touched her naked wrist, she might have lost her mind. Instead, she lifted her chin and took a step back. He stepped forward.

"I've missed you," he said.

"That's why we're here – the girls, I mean. They really wanted to see you."

"And your pool," giggled Lucy.

"Touching," said Alex, stroking Lucy's hair and gazing wistfully at his more skeptical family members. "You got my letters, right?"

"I did," Meredith said calmly. "They were – I don't know." She lowered her chin. "Confusing."

"Don't be confused," Alex said. "I'm not. Not anymore."

"But you're still here," said Meredith.

"Working," said Alex.

"Where's your wife?"

Alex swallowed. "She's home. I thought you would be happy to see me."

"We are happy to see you," said Maggie. "But it doesn't matter what you say. It's what you do."

Meredith looked into Alex's pleading eyes. She felt herself responding, all the old synapses reconnecting as her heart fell toward his arms, his mouth. No. She had a will, she had self control. But her body was softening, leaning towards him. No. She stood here with her children, on the edge of something, a ledge, a cliff, and she still couldn't tell if it were love or death. She would not lose her footing, and she wouldn't let him push her. Maggie was right. Alex had to prove himself with more than a handful of lovely letters and a few days off.

"Well, take good care of them," she said. She reached down and gave each of her daughters a hug and a kiss. "Have fun, you two. I'll be at Grandma's. I'll pick you up on Saturday, so you can spend some time with her too."

"What does she have to do?" asked Lucy.

"I think she has all the ice cream cones you can eat," said Meredith.

"Okay," said Lucy. "I can do that. As long as you take me to Disney first," she said, turning to Alex.

"I can do that," he said. He took Lucy's moist palm and Maggie's cool one, winked at Meredith, and turned toward baggage claim.

Between a wetlands pond and a divided highway, the twelve stories of Independence Valley, An Active Retirement Community, loomed before Meredith like the Ghost of Thanksgiving Future. An automatic door divided the thick air outside from artificial autumn. In the lobby, a fake oak tree dropped plastic leaves onto a cotton mat that was supposed to look like snow. An inflatable turkey in a Pilgrim hat grinned near the elevators. Meredith nodded to a white-haired woman gripping the handles of a rakish walker, decorated prematurely with tinsel and candy canes. They entered the elevators, and Meredith pushed ten.

"What floor would you like?" she asked the woman.

"Oh, no floor, Dear, thank you. I just like to go up and down."

This would have been sad if the woman weren't so content. She was living for the moment, Meredith decided, not fretting over future goals or problems. Maybe she had discovered the meaning of life – you might as well enjoy the ride.

"Look, you can see the people in Assisted Living."

It was a glass elevator. Meredith looked down at the tiny old folks in tiny wheelchairs with tiny caregivers on the third floor below. "Is that where you live?" she asked.

"Certainly not!" said the lady indignantly. Thankfully, the elevator door opened. Meredith nodded and scooted into the hallway.

Independence Valley, a refurbished Embassy Suites Hotel, had circular hallways dotted with apartment doors on one side, and on the other, an enormous drop into a large atrium. Meredith wondered if any of its residents, sick of a refrigerated old age, ever pitched over the railing to end it all in the Lucite shrubbery below. But, to their credit, people could adjust to almost anything, and living here was safe, reasonably comfortable, and, as Meredith knew from conversations with her mother, filled with intrigue. She knocked on her mother's front door, decorated with a felt squirrel holding an acorn and a mezuzah.

Sara Greenfeld opened the door and threw her arms around her daughter's elbows. Sara had never been tall, but in the last decade she had shrunk considerably. If this trend continued, by the time she was ninety her gray bouffant would reach only to Meredith's knees.

"Sweetheart! I'm so glad you're here! Come in! I'll make some tea."

At age seventy-five, Sara was always cold. She wore two sweaters, a vest, a wool skirt, and thick, dark stockings, despite the sun streaming into the tiny apartment through the bedroom window. Her back bent, and Meredith knew that it hurt her. Nevertheless, Sara bustled into the kitchen, tucked cinnamon bread into the toaster, and stuck two teacups of water into the microwave. Sara lived on tea and toast and aspirin.

"Now, you sit down," Sara called, although Meredith was only three feet away, in the living room. "I want to hear all about your trip and the girls, everything."

It was true, Sara did want to hear it all, every detail. She was the only person in the world who would be in the least interested, let alone incensed, to learn that the man in front of Meredith had pushed his seat back during the flight.

"So rude! People are so thoughtless!" Sara exclaimed indignantly, setting Meredith's snack on a TV tray next to the sofa. Sara stooped and then collapsed with a small bump onto her favorite chair. "Now, what else can I bring you? Do you have a napkin? Do you need some jelly?"

"No, Mom, this is perfect," Meredith said. And actually, it was. She took a breath and plunged in. "Alex met us – the girls – at the airport."

"Well, I should hope so," said Sara, buttering her toast. "After you brought his daughters all this way. But I'm glad you did. We'll have such a nice Thanksgiving together. In fact, it's," Sara looked at her watch, "in two hours."

Meredith was shocked. "Really? It's only Monday."

"I know, it's ridiculous," said Sara. "But I guess the cooks and whatnot like to be with their own families on the day itself, so they give us our dinner today. It's not very good, either," she confided. "But they like to think they're doing something nice for us, so we humor them along."

At four o'clock, Meredith took her mother's elbow and helped her to the elevator. They plunged down to the lobby, where grinning staff members beckoned them to a large round table in the dining area.

"Same old rolls," commented Sara, as Meredith pulled out her chair.

Soon, six other senior ladies with matching stiff hairdos joined them at the table. Meredith had noticed the lobby beauty parlor, undoubtedly the culprit. All of the women dressed as her mother did, in winter clothes from their younger days in the North. Proudly, Sara introduced her daughter to her friends. Meredith nodded and pulled her own sweater close.

"It's freezing, isn't it, Dear," noted Millie, on Meredith's left. "It's not like we haven't complained."

"You'd think it would be cheaper to use less air conditioning," said Meredith.

"It's like living in a morgue," said Bella, across from her. "If no one notices we're dead, they can keep collecting rent." A large woman in an Indian headdress set a plate of iceberg lettuce topped with Thousand Island dressing in front of Meredith. Bella turned to Sara. "So nice that your daughter could come visit you," she said.

"Do you have any children?" asked Meredith.

"Oh, yes, two sons. Sons are worthless," she said. "Men run the world, and their wives are busy with the children and their own parents. They figure their husbands will see to their own mothers, but they're wrong. I was the same way, and I'm sorry about it now. But daughters – you're lucky, Sara."

"Daughters don't always get along with their mothers," said Meredith. "Especially teenage girls, they are the worst. Was I awful, Mom?"

"I don't remember that," said Sara, blotting her mouth daintily. "You were always marvelous."

Meredith laughed. "Well, I was the only one. Teenage girls can be pretty rough on their mothers. I've seen that a lot in my line of work."

"Meredith is a lawyer, she's a prosecutor," said Sara.

"We know," said Sylvia. "That must be so interesting. Do teenagers ever actually kill their mothers?"

"Oh, Sylvia!" said Sara, shocked. She turned to her daughter. "Well, do they?"

"Not in my neck of the woods," said Meredith. "They may blame their moms for putting too much pressure on them, like to go to the right college, or to be skinny, something like that, but I haven't seen that actually push anyone to murder."

Meredith stopped. Suddenly, she felt unsettled. A young Hispanic man with cardboard buckles taped to his belt and shoes removed their salads and set down their dinner plates. Everything except the turkey had been served with an ice cream scoop.

"It's always hard to eat someone else's stuffing," said Millie.

"Yes, well. Speaking of murder, did you hear the ambulance yesterday?" asked Bella.

"Why, yes," said Sara. "But I didn't think anything of it."

"Well, you wouldn't," said Bella. "But – do you see Victor anywhere?" She paused dramatically. Meredith poked her mashed potato ball as the others looked around the dining area. "That's because he's dead!"

"Bella, this isn't very nice dinner conversation," said Sara. "Anyway, it's too bad, but it's not so surprising. He must have been ninety years old."

"Ninety-three," said Bella. "The Powers That Be are trying to hush it up, but I heard that the police think it wasn't natural causes. There might be an investigation."

"What happened to him?" asked Meredith.

"Well, he was very sick, I'll give you that," said Bella. "They just don't know if he was That Sick. And his family wants him cremated, and you know he wouldn't have wanted that. That's always suspicious."

"Why wouldn't he have wanted it?" asked Sara. She put down her fork. "I want that."

Meredith looked at her mother. Her hand was shaking, and she had barely touched her slice of cranberry sauce. Meredith put her arm around her mother's thin shoulders. "So," she said brightly, "let me tell you about my problem. I would like some advice. My husband and I are divorced, he left me for a younger woman about five years ago. I know, the same old story, what a fool. They moved here for a year, to Orlando, and he's been writing me these – love letters." They were love letters, Meredith thought, though she hadn't described them that way to herself until now. "What do you think I should do?"

The women were riveted, and they all had advice, all contradicting each other. Sara picked up her fork, speared an edge of turkey, and raised it to her mouth. If that were her reward for embarrassing herself, it was worth it.

"And we remember those we love who are no longer with us, and we thank you for giving us good friends and good company on this Thanksgiving Day."

Susie raised her chardonnay in a toast and surveyed her table, like a centerfold from *Better Homes and Gardens*. She had even bought a cornucopia made out of bread and filled it with tangerines and grapes. And she had roasted the Butterball herself – you just rinsed it and stuck it in the oven until the plastic timer popped up, she did that every year. The stuffing was her mother's recipe, stale Wonder Bread cut in cubes, tossed with butter and salt and pepper, and smashed into the cavity so that it turned into a damp, fatty mush. Mindy made cranberry sauce and biscuits from scratch, and Ron brought sweet potatoes with marshmallows as a joke, and also a pumpkin pie. He said he liked cooking orange gourds and root vegetables, though the pie looked suspiciously professional.

"Mindy, please pass the butter to Lauren," Susie said. She knew Lauren didn't want any butter, but she should express an interest in Lauren, for Ron's sake. Having him here was such a blessing, after the last terrible two months of Joel being dead.

"This looks beautiful, Mrs. Steinmetz," said Lauren. She had a tiny strand of everything on her plate and was poking it with her dessert fork.

"I'm glad you're enjoying it, Dear. So, how is college?"

"It's okay," said Lauren, narrowing her eyes. "But I'm glad to be home for a few days, as it turns out. I'm kind of surprised about that."

"I think Mindy feels that way too. Don't you, Mindy?" Susie looked pointedly at her daughter, who was enjoying her marshmallows. Susie could have fit two Laurens into Mindy's jeans and still had room for a drumstick.

"Sure," said Mindy. "I like school, but my roommates are morons, though they do go home most weekends to their farms to do their laundry on the old scrub board. It's nice to be in my own room again." She speared a drippy cucumber and popped it in her mouth.

"So," said Lauren, looking back and forth between Ron and Susie. "This is cozy." She set down her fork and pursed her lips.

"It was very kind of Mrs.Steinmetz to invite us for Thanksgiving."

Ron was awfully handsome, in his blue blazer and lemon dress shirt, the top button nattily unfastened. After two months of scuffing around the house in slippers, sweatpants, and Joel's old flannel shirt, Susie was glad she had made an effort today. When she crossed her high-heeled legs under the table, her skirt hiked up, and she glanced at Ron.

"You girls have been friends for, well, years," Ron continued, nodding at Lauren and Mindy. "It's about time our families got to know each other. And I really liked Joel." He glanced at Susie. "It's too bad your mother didn't get to know Mindy's parents better."

"And she would be super excited that, while she's barely cold in the grave, you're having such an awesome time with Her." Lauren stared belligerently at Susie. "You really bounced back, Dad. A real lesson in resilience. Yeah, I bet she and Mom would have gotten along great."

"What's that supposed to mean?" asked Mindy, wiping French dressing off her chin. "Because your mother was so perfect, and we're not?"

"No. Mom was not perfect," said Lauren. "You certainly know that, Dad. She wasn't exactly thrilled with either one of us."

"Families disagree," said Ron. "It's because we care enough about each other to be honest."

"Ha, don't make me laugh. But I did love Mom. In spite of everything." Lauren started to sniffle. Ron put his hand on the back of her chair and looked embarrassed. "Yeah, right," she said. "Like you care about me." Lauren flung back her arm and whacked him hard in the chest. Startled, he dropped his hand, and he looked like he might hit her back.

Susie stood up. "I'm going to put the coffee on. Mindy, come help me. Excuse us."

In the kitchen, Susie flipped open the coffeemaker and turned to Mindy. "This is supposed to be a nice holiday dinner, and Lauren is ruining it. What is going on with her?"

"I don't know," said Mindy, shrugging. "I guess she misses her mom. This is their first Thanksgiving without her. Maybe seeing you and her dad together – it feels weird."

"I don't know what you mean by 'together," said Susie. "There is nothing going on between me and Mr. Block. He was a friend of your father's, and Lauren is a friend of yours. And I didn't want to be alone, just the two of us. It would have been sad."

"I know, Mom. And I know nothing's going on. I mean, Dad just died, and anyway, you guys are old."

Susie stared at Mindy. "I mean, he is old, he must be twenty years older than you."

"Well, not twenty," Susie said primly. She touched her red curls and measured coffee into the filter basket. "Anyway, he just lost his wife. I am trying to be nice here. And I am trying not to get depressed. I think Lauren is just being difficult to distract us from the fact that she doesn't eat anything."

"She is super thin," said Mindy. "Must be nice."

"There is nothing nice about it, especially if it gives her that sassy attitude." Susie reached around and gave Mindy a squeeze. "I'm proud of you. I know none of this is easy, but you just carry on. You can always lose those extra pounds later, when you're feeling better."

"Thanks, Mom. I guess."

Susie took the plastic wrap off the pumpkin pie, pulled a can of Reddi-wip out of the refrigerator, and sailed into the dining room. Lauren was sniffing and wiping her eyes, while her father faced front and looked uncomfortable. "So, the traditional Thanksgiving dessert!" Susie announced, setting the can down on the table with a flourish. "The coffee will be ready in a moment, and then I expect everyone," she paused and raised her eyebrows at Lauren, "to have a nice big piece of this lovely pie."

Mindy sat down. Ron stood, gathered the dinner plates, and followed Susie into the kitchen. "This has been so nice. Thank you for inviting us. I don't know what we would have done without you."

"Well, I'm sure you would have done fine," said Susie, flushing. "I'm sure you have lots of friends who would have been glad to have you over."

"Not so many," said Ron, scraping Lauren's plate into the garbage disposal while Susie pulled saucers from the cupboard. "We used to eat Thanksgiving dinner at the Club. This is really much nicer."

"Sweet of you to say so. Marcia didn't cook?" She busied herself with the dishwasher.

"Not on Thanksgiving," he said. "I know it's a home kind of holiday, but that was our tradition. But I wasn't sure what to do this year, without her. It's good to shake things up a little, and to be with friends."

"Yes," said Susie. "I hope Lauren will be okay."

"I have to admit, sometimes I feel like throttling her. She isn't easy, and her mother used to handle all of her moods. Now it's up to me, and – well, we've never been close, and frankly, I'm not the soul of patience myself."

"I don't believe that. I think you're a planner. I admire that."

Ron smiled. "Yes, I am a planner. Part of being a lawyer, I guess." He stopped. "It's a lot to get used to in one year, a lot of big changes. It's just going to take time, but soon, everyone will adjust."

"I hope so," said Susie, lifting the coffee pot and leading Ron back to the dining room.

Chapter Twelve

Meredith always enjoyed the aftermath of a vacation. She liked dumping the suitcase into the washer and folding clean clothes. She liked sorting the mail into junk, bills, and better piles and throwing all the junk in the recycling bin. Best of all, she liked going to the grocery store and refilling the fridge from its last-dimpled-apple-and-frayed-lettuce-leaf stage to a homey, rooted plenty. She liked everything about nesting, except making dinner. And tonight, she didn't have to make it.

"Why are we having turkey again? I'm sick of it," whined Lucy, stabbing a slab of white meat like a belligerent Neanderthal .

"Yeah, Mom, we already had it twice," said Maggie. "You said we'd get pizza."

"That was before I knew that Grandma had – given us this gift." Upon opening her suitcase to unpack, Meredith had discovered multiple Ziploc bags containing foil-wrapped packages of food – turkey, sweet potatoes, stuffing, cauliflower, and an entire pumpkin pie. Somehow, the frail old lady had sneaked leftovers from the dinner they had cooked on Thanksgiving Day into Meredith's luggage. Having travelled from the chilly retirement home to the cargo hold of a jet to the trunk of a cab at the end of a Chicago November, the leftovers were still cool and hopefully botulism-free when Meredith discovered them. From beneath her dirty clothes bag, she also unearthed a jar of strawberry jam marked down to eighty-nine cents, a pair of terry cloth slippers, and an expired Manischewitz cake mix. Somewhere in her tiny apartment, her mother stored enough bargains to withstand nuclear winter, and she was liberal about sharing them with loved ones.

"So," Meredith said, picking at a turkey wing, "are you ready for school tomorrow?"

Maggie rolled her eyes. "Are you sure we won't get sick from this?"

"Shawna was sick," offered Lucy. "She didn't eat any turkey at all."

"That's too bad," said Meredith. "What was wrong with her?" She cut open her sweet potato.

"We don't know exactly," said Lucy. "She wouldn't go on Space Mountain. Dad said she was a little under the weather, but she would feel better soon, and we should just act like she wasn't there."

Well, that sounded like Alex. Despite his resolution to give their marriage a chance in Florida, acting like Shawna wasn't there continued to be his MO. Oddly, Meredith wasn't sure how she felt about that.

After some half-hearted pumpkin pie and dishes, Meredith turned to the mail she had dropped in a heap on the coffee table. Sitting on the couch, she sorted – ComEd bill, American Cancer Society – they wanted money, but they included free address labels, so that went in the good pile. Stuck between the Land's End catalog and *Cosmo* – she bought it for the articles – was a long white envelope with Alex's return address. She had just seen him. Why was he writing so soon?

November 23, 1997

Dear Meredith,

I am at the pool with Maggie and Lucy. We played some of our favorite games - Marco Polo, crab races, and Jumping Olympics. The waitress just brought them lemonades with umbrellas and a basket of French fries - sorry, Mom - and, lounging on deck chairs and munching, they look like they are to-the-manor-born. Must be from their Kenilworth years. Ha ha, not so funny, I know.

You know - well, maybe you don't, you never asked - I rented out the Kenilworth house, I didn't sell it. So, I'll be moving back there in the spring, right around the time Maggie finishes 8th grade. The house is so close to New Trier, and I have this fantasy that we could all live there - makes sense, so convenient! - and think how happy we would be. I know you like your little house in Wilmette, but how do you get to New Trier from there? I think it's impossible.

Where was Shawna in this idyllic scenario, Meredith wondered. Well, maybe she shouldn't worry about that. Shawna apparently would vanish, and Meredith and the girls would move back in with Alex, as if the last five years had never happened. Or could he possibly mean they would all live there, as in Shawna too?

I was so happy to see you, even for those brief minutes at the airport. You are so beautiful to me, so smart and giving, and so pretty, even after all those hours on the plane and bundled up in your old down coat. I just miss you so much.

I know you worry about the Shawna factor - you are so good, who else in your place would worry about her feelings? - but I think that I just need to let her go. I can't hang on to something that isn't working, it isn't fair to anyone. She likes it down here, I can imagine her choosing to stay in Florida. Maybe we'll be lucky, and she'll find a new man in the next few months, and everyone will be happy. Whatever happens, we will be rid of her. Well, that sounds harsh -- I will not let her be an impediment. There has been too much suffering already.

So, I am thinking about the future, our future together. I am going to make it happen. We will be together, if it is up to me.

All my love,

Alex

Meredith looked at the letter again. It was certainly romantic. Maybe the sun had fried his brain. He would get rid of Shawna? What was he talking about? Lucy said that Shawna was sick, and Alex wasn't the least bit concerned. He was done with her. Now he just wanted her to disappear.

Alex was a doctor. He had access to medications, and he knew how to make people well – and also how to make them sick, and then some. And he was performing mad scientist experiments which, granted, she might understand if she ever asked him to explain his research. She imagined Dr. Alexander Frankenstein in his lab, some crazy poisoning guy with bubbling liquids cycling through curly tubes into smoking vials. But that was nuts, Alex was, well, Alex. He didn't necessarily have it all together, but basically he was – sweet. He wasn't perfect, and she still wasn't sure she could trust him, but – she shook her head. She clearly had seen too many Svengooli movies. Nobody she loved would ever physically injure their own spouse. Why would anyone do that, in the age of no-fault divorce? Especially not Alex, and especially not for her.

"Girls, you need to take your showers and get ready for bed," she called. Tomorrow they would get back to the old routine. They had spent enough time in Fantasyland.

"Is it wrong to celebrate the fact that our daughters are gone?" Ron asked, opening the car door for Susie.

She beamed at him. "Not when they'll be back so soon for Christmas break. Anyway, they're having fun. Well, exams. But I'll bet they're having fun anyway. Why shouldn't we?" She stepped into the black Mercedes.

Ron stared appreciatively before closing the door. Susie's red hair flared like a sparkler, and her fair freckled cheeks looked like cinnamon sugar cookies. Settling into the bucket seat, she gave a demure tug to her chocolate skirt and crossed her matching boots. Ron rounded the car, slid into the driver's seat, and grabbed the gear shift. As he swiveled to look out the rear window, he caught her eye, and she smiled again. Her lips were perfect pink bows.

"So, where are we going?" Susie asked.

"It's a surprise," Ron said, revving the engine. Relaxing, she sat quietly, staring out the window. Ron hoped he wasn't moving too fast, asking her out only two months – well, almost three months – since Joel died. His death had upset Susie much more than Ron expected. Joel had been such a drag on her, he had thought it would be more of a relief. He wound through the neighborhood and down the entrance ramp to the expressway, heading toward the city.

"I hope you're okay with this," Ron said, entering the traffic flow. "I just wanted to thank you for Thanksgiving."

"Oh," said Susie. Was she a little downcast? She hesitated, then unleashed that brilliant grin. "Well, thank you. It's nice of you."

"Not so nice," said Ron. "I wanted to spend some time with you too."

"Well, that is very nice," she said.

Ron pushed a button on the steering wheel. A soft rock station started playing "Yesterday." Great. He left it. It was a pretty song.

Susie started giggling. "Remember that song about the boy getting hit by a train – or was he drag racing – 'Teen Angel,' is that it?"

"Or, what about 'the day that Billie Joe Macalester jumped off the Tallahatchie Bridge?'" offered Ron. "Why all the songs about accidents and suicides?"

"I guess teenagers don't usually die of cancer," said Susie.

"Nobody falls through a glass table." He paused. "Except Marcia."

Susie started laughing again, but he was afraid that in a minute she would start to cry. Ron pushed another button on the steering wheel and changed the station. Dogs were ruffing "Jingle Bells."

"Better?" Ron asked.

Susie reached across the gear shift and put her hand lightly on his thigh. The feeling was electric, a vibrating wave that zapped to his groin, so vivid he could almost see it. No one had touched him like that since Marcia died seven months ago. And he was so accustomed to Marcia, they had been married for twenty-five years. He still felt something when she touched him, but it was more like activating a well-used pathway. She knew the buttons to push for an efficient anatomical reaction. It was satisfying, he had liked it fine. But this was something else.

"I hate Christmas music," Susie said. "But that's okay, leave this one. It's funny."

"When they start singing about mangers, I'll change it."

"Perfect," said Susie. She took her hand away.

They exited at Ohio Street. Susie sat patiently. She didn't try to guess where they were going – he had thought she might, as a game. And she didn't try to argue him into telling, which Marcia would have done. Marcia liked control, she liked to plan things and to know what was going on. Ron understood that, he was the same way. But she couldn't control everything. The way her life ended was her biggest surprise of all.

Ron drove east to Michigan Avenue. "Oh, look, it's beautiful," said Susie. "The one good thing about Christmas is the lights."

It was beautiful. They drove north, between high rises rimmed with tree branches twinkling with lights. Taxis whipped around them, edging Ron out of the right lane, and the traffic lights stopped them every other block for an endless display of turning arrows and walk signs. But Ron didn't care. Even the slow, weaving cars of lost tourists and the legless homeless men propped in wheelchairs were wonderful to him now. Why had he never noticed before?

Ron glided up to the entrance of the Ritz Hotel. Valets in navy wool coats and caps like sea captains swarmed the Mercedes and opened both doors. Susie stepped out and joined him on the sidewalk, under a heat lamp. "Have you eaten in the Ritz Dining Room before?"

Susie caught her breath. "No, but I hear it's gorgeous. That's awfully extravagant, in exchange for a Butterball."

"I wanted to do something special," Ron said. As she walked into the elevator, he placed his hand lightly on her back.

They stepped out of the elevator onto a sculpted carpet. A large lobby opened before them, with a circular fountain bouncing a thousand shoots of water into the air. They passed the café, where hotel guests sipped glasses of chardonnay with tiny, expensive salads. Down a long hallway, they walked over a curved bridge into the spell of the Dining Room. The walnut walls were warm, low lamps flickered like candles, and everything glowed. Susie and Ron were relieved of their coats, and the maitre d' led them up a couple of steps to a cozy banquette.

144

"I'll sit next to you," said Ron. "If you don't mind."

"That sounds perfect," said Susie.

The room shimmered, and Susie herself seemed to emanate light and heat. Marcia would have worn a black sweater or a shawl, but Susie's bare arms extended from her glittery tank top, her collarbone cradling a strand of pearls.

"You look lovely," Ron said. "I'm sorry. I can't help myself."

Susie touched his cheek with her index finger, a gesture both intimate and revelatory. "It's hard to dress appropriately when you don't know where you're going," she said. "I'm glad you approve."

This was supposed to be a surprise for Susie, but she had amazed him. She was quite an awesome woman, he thought. Maybe he hadn't permitted himself to see her when they first met, but now he could see everything clearly. They had been through a terrible time, but he was alive, and so was she. They had helped each other through horror, and now he could see the beauty of the world again. When Marcia died, nothing made sense. But here was Susie, in the same situation. Their daughters were even best friends. Ron didn't know if he believed in God. He certainly hadn't after Marcia died. But if crossing paths with Susie were an accident, it was a lucky one.

Ron raised a glass of champagne. "L'Chaim!" he said.

"Yes, please," said Susie.

WINTER

Chapter Thirteen

February 1998

Snow blew in jagged streaks across the pavement, as hunched cars lurched through the dark, congested streets of downtown Highland Park. Clutching the steering wheel, Meredith scanned the angled lane to her right for empty parking spaces and tail lights, but the parked cars, coated with a thick layer of snow, seemed camped for the duration. In the pioneer spirit – so, it was snowing, it was February in Chicago, put on some clothes and get over it – Meredith had crawled up Green Bay Road in a minor storm for fast food and a cheap movie with her daughters on Saturday night. What she couldn't understand was why everyone else was as big an idiot as she was. People, you could be home, safe and cozy in your pajama pants with a bowl of popcorn and a video! Instead, the entire North Shore seemed to be cycling through Highland Park like dirty socks in a detergent blizzard.

Finally settled in a spot of questionable legality several blocks from ground zero, the three Bennett girls scurried down the slippery sidewalk, across salted streets and slush heaps, and into the bright frenzy of Michael's Red Hots. Unzipping her coat, Meredith wiped her glasses on the shirt under her sweater and scanned the menu board. Beside her, Maggie and Lucy were two shivering, snow-encrusted stacks of knitwear.

"Do you know what you want?" asked Meredith, though she didn't know why she bothered. After much hedging and waffling, they always ordered the same thing. "You know what? Why don't you two get ketchup and all that stuff, and get us a table. I'll take care of this."

The two mounds of daughter hurried toward what was hopefully the warmer back room. Meredith entered the fray of ordering -- char dogs and charburgers first, then toppings – pickles and onions and even sauerkraut – then French fries, sodas, and payment. The linoleum floor was slushy, but the heat of the grill and the stress of jostling other windblown parents and their hungry, snotty offspring warmed her blood. By the time she toted her loaded tray past the ketchup counter and into the rear, she thought she might be able to take off her coat.

Maggie and Lucy were at a table towards the back, under the disco ball (for Bar Mitzvah parties), and next to the arcade area. Meredith sat on a plastic chair. It was still cold. She shoved char dogs and Cokes at Maggie and Lucy and set the fry basket in the middle on a napkin, in case of spillage. Then she looked around the room.

Most tables, like her own, contained adults – parents, or martyred grandparents – and minors in winter outfits and stages of ketchup incrustation. Toddlers in boots and snowsuits sat stuffed into highchairs surrounded by bits of roll and soda straws. Teenagers, refusing to allow a cold snap to spoil their look, wore tee shirts, sneakers, and frayed jeans, with jaunty knit caps their only concession to the cold. But amid this sea of families sat one adults-only couple, oblivious to the chill and the chaos, eyes only for each other. Meredith thought they looked familiar, or at least the man did. She peered at them more closely, and when that didn't help, she stood and walked past them, ostensibly to check out the Samurai Showdown 2 game on the back wall. Yes, she was right. The man was Ron Block. And the babe with him – well, she was kind of a mom-babe, with wild red hair and a surprisingly snug, low-veed sweater for the weather and general ambience.

Having studied the Samurais sufficiently, Meredith resumed her seat. Swinging her boots while concentrating on her dinner, Lucy was rhythmically kicking Maggie in the knee. While this did not appear to concern or deter Lucy, Maggie was beginning to raise her voice.

"Lucy, cut it out! I mean it!" she growled, her timbre rising at the end toward a shriek.

Fortunately, this environment was like space, where no one could hear you scream. "Lucy, quit kicking. Maggie, here, take my seat."

Maggie moved over, and Meredith sat on the opposite end, allowing Lucy to kick obliviously as she munched. So, how long had Mrs. Block been dead? Meredith struggled for milestones. She definitely died last year, Maggie was in her seventh grade math class. It must have been spring, the weather was beautiful that funeral day, and Maggie had a substitute teacher for just another month or so – end of April, beginning of May?

149

And now it was mid-February, so a good nine months. Okay, that might be a quasi-legitimate amount of time – but was this a Valentine's Day date? Having Valentine's Day dinner at Michael's was either the worst or the most romantic idea Meredith had ever heard. The way those two were looking at each other, it didn't matter where they were. Look, he was blotting her ketchuppy mouth with his napkin! Oh, no, she didn't just dab his nose with mustard? No, she didn't, they were adults after all. Meredith wanted to stay to see if they floated out of the restaurant in slow motion, but she had to get over to the Highland Park Theater to see "George of the Jungle." At least the jungle would look warm.

Maybe she should go over to say hello. After all, Meredith knew Ron Block, she had been a guest in his home. Certainly, he hated her, but he was under a lot of stress then, that was water under the bridge, or glass on the tumbled marble. And wasn't it nice that he was happy now! It had only been nine months, but they said that widowers with happy marriages wanted to get married again a.s.a.p. But the Block's marriage had not been happy, at least not according to their daughter Lauren. Lauren, who had bravely visited Meredith at work to report her suspicions of her father, and whom Meredith had turned away with lame reassurances. But married couples did fight. It didn't mean that they pushed each other through glass tables, and it didn't mean they couldn't have accidents. Still, it seemed a little strange. Who was this leprechaun-siren? Had Ron known her before Marcia died?

"Mom, we need to go," said Maggie, pulling her Turtle Fur over her ears.

150

"Just a minute, I'll be right back. I want to say hello to Mr. Block over there," said Meredith, nodding in his direction.

Maggie took a look. "Who?"

"You know, Mr. Block, Mrs. Block's husband."

"Dead Mrs. Block – Mom, you don't even know him. We're going to miss the previews," said Maggie.

"I have to go to the bathroom," announced Lucy, now that all of her outdoor gear was securely fastened.

"Okay, fine," Meredith conceded. "We better leave, you can go to the bathroom when we get there." For all she knew, "George of the Jungle" was the perfect Valentines date flick, and she didn't want to end up on the front row.

After the movie, which had not been terrible, Meredith wormed her way down a slick but salted Green Bay Road. The fantasy tropical paradise seemed to have stunned her children into silence, allowing Meredith to focus on the road and her own thoughts, which returned to Ron Block as they spun through Glencoe on their way south. So, he had a girlfriend. That wasn't illegal. He was probably lonely, especially with Lauren in college now. And the woman, although cute in a spunky mom sort of way, violated the trophy rule – she looked a bit older than half Ron's age plus seven. Not that it mattered, he could date whomever he pleased, and it would still be None of Meredith's Business.

This weather was terrible. Why was Valentine's Day in the winter? Shouldn't lovebirds be flitting around, flowers popping up, little things growing? Maybe St. Valentine was executed on an icy February

151

14, shot through the heart with a blazing arrow. That would explain a lot of things.

Meredith parked the car – phew, the family had left the house and lived, a winter victory – and picked her way along the back path in an effort not to slip on the ice under the snow. Trailing behind, Maggie and Lucy were waking up, the brisk wind slapping their cheeks a stinging pink. In the front hall, Meredith hung coats and scarves and gathered the mail from the floor. Three large pink envelopes stood out from the bills and the ads for Marshall Fields' One Day Sale, This Friday and Saturday Only.

"Maggie, Lucy, looks like you got Valentines from Dad," she said, walking into the kitchen to distribute two of the pink envelopes to her daughters, whose dessert-seeking heads were buried in the freezer.

And the biggest, pinkest envelope was for her. Trying not to be overly dramatic, but wanting privacy, she took it upstairs to her bedroom and sat down on her bed. Their bed.

Yes, she had kept their bed, hers and Alex's. Well, she wasn't going to let Shawna sleep in it, and there was no reason to throw out a perfectly good mattress. Of course, they had conceived their daughters on this bed and had some lovely, intimate times here, but Meredith was not being sentimental. She was practical, that was all. She gave the bed a friendly pat and stroked the floral quilt that a law school friend had given them for a wedding present. The darn thing wouldn't wear out, that was all! They must make them out of woven plastic bound up with chemicals, just like bread these days, which never went stale. Maggie and Lucy would probably bury her in it.

Meredith inserted her finger under the envelope flap and ripped it open. She pulled out a large, embossed card featuring a bouquet of raised white roses beside curly gold letters spelling *"Happy Valentine's Day Across the Miles."* It looked like something you would give your mother. She opened it. The printed message read, *"Although we are far apart, you are always near to my heart. Happy Valentine's Day, with love."* Alex had signed it. And he had inserted a lock of hair, tied in the middle with a pink ribbon, like a mustache for a little girl. Was she supposed to wear it in a locket, like a Victorian wife waiting for her seafaring husband's ship to come in? This game had gone on long enough. Meredith picked up the phone and punched in Alex's cell phone number. Thank God for cell phones. At least she could be pretty sure that Shawna wouldn't answer.

"Hello?" Alex said groggily.

"Oh, whoops. I forgot about the time change. Sorry." Meredith was only a little sorry. After all, he was the one who had moved two thousand miles away. "I got your Valentine. Thank you. Alex, we need to talk."

She could hear rustling, as Alex presumably exited the marital bed and skulked down the hall. "What's going on?" he asked from some safe distance.

"Alex, you keep sending me these – lovely messages, and I don't know what to think."

"Meredith, Dear – I want you back, that's all."

She could hear his breath, but she couldn't feel it. "Alex, this is serious. It isn't just the two of us. There are other people involved."

"Believe me, I know that, probably even better than you do," he said. "But I don't care. I mean, I care, but I have to be with you. I miss you. You are my family."

"First, I have to know you are serious. You can't yank my chain and then leave again. I couldn't take it. And the girls – if you come back, it has to be for good. Your letters have been sweet, but I don't know if I can trust you. Look what you are doing to Shawna."

"I know, I made a terrible mistake, and I am so, so sorry. But I want to come back. I have learned my lesson."

He sounded like a contrite little boy who wanted his own way. And the problem, of course, was that she loved him. She still loved him. In spite of everything, she had never stopped. She actually felt concerned about him. But she couldn't allow this to continue, as flattering and exciting as it was for her, unless she knew it was real.

"Alex, we need to talk. I need to see you – alone, in person. I need to see your face, we need to discuss this. It's too important. I don't want there to be any mistakes, any misunderstandings. Can you come up here?" He could fly up tomorrow, make a grand gesture. That would be something, then she would know she was important.

"Sweetheart, I can't get away. My research – it's in a delicate place right now, I need to be here." He paused. A tear welled in her eye. Nothing had changed. This was just like before. "Please understand. I know this sounds like me putting you off, but I'm not. Look, I wasn't planning to come home until May, but I am going to make it earlier – I have been thinking about this, I don't want to stay away a minute longer than I have to. I think that if I work night and day, I can finish up here and be home -- with you -- next month. I'm talking four or five more weeks, that's all, and then I would be back for good. Then we could talk face-to-face every day, until I convince you that I have changed, that we belong together."

Meredith wiped her cheek. "Next month?"

"Yes," he said. "I'm going to work my butt off, and I will be back. I promise."

"What about Shawna – in the meantime? Are you two still – together?"

Alex paused. "That is a delicate situation. You are going to have to trust me on that."

Meredith didn't say anything. She just hung up.

As if eighth grade weren't bad enough, what with mean girls writing anonymous letters to former friends saying they were fat or that their boobs were too big, and having to step around the prone bodies of boys punching each other on the linoleum as she hurried to French class, and of course the flour sack baby that she had accidentally killed by forgetting it in the freezing car overnight, Maggie was now enduring the ultimate eighth grade hurdle: the Holocaust unit. She had excused herself to the bathroom during the shower scene in "Schindler's List" – she needed to change her sanitary napkin anyway – oh yeah, there was that too. And she quickly passed along the educational books with pictures of women that could be her mother, and children that could be her, only more old-fashioned, standing in front of cattle cars. She supposed they needed to know this stuff, and to some kids it was ancient history. For her, it was personal.

"If you had one Jewish grandparent, that was good enough for the Nazis. It didn't matter what you believed, how much you blended into German society. You were Jewish, and you were a problem," announced their Social Studies teacher, Mrs. Baker. Wide-eyed, all the Rosenblums and Goldsteins looked at each other. Maggie stared down at her desk.

Maggie didn't know what she believed. Her mother was Greenfeld, and her father wasn't. She didn't go to church, but she didn't have a Bat Mitzvah either. She and Lucy got presents on Chanukah and Christmas, which other kids thought made her extra lucky. When she asked her parents what she was, they said that she could choose. And so, she was nothing. With extra gifts. But apparently, according to some people, she didn't have a choice. She was toast, and so was her grandma in Florida, and Lucy, and her mom. If the Nazis came again, which, of course, they wouldn't. But they had to learn all this horrible stuff. Just In Case.

At eleven o'clock, Maggie knocked quietly on her mom's bedroom door. "Yes, come in," Meredith said.

Maggie opened the door. Propped on two pillows stamped with red and green snowflakes against a creamy background, her mother looked fragile. In motion she always seemed so strong, like she could handle anything all by herself. That was one of the things that made her so annoying. But now she looked tired, with her Walgreens half glasses perched on her nose, a spray of delicate lines branching from the corner of each eye, a

156

dusted curl on her temple. She held a book propped on her old quilt, and the bedside lamp lit her like a ghost. The bed was large, queen-sized, but she lay on one side of it, as she always had, her father's side empty and waiting.

"What is it, Honey?" Meredith asked, putting down her book. "Can't you sleep? Come here."

Maggie walked up to her mother, who scooted to the middle of the bed and patted the warmed-up spot beside her. She wasn't a baby, some two-year-old who needed to get in bed with her mom – but it was cold, in her tee shirt and pajama pants and bare feet. She sat on the edge of the bed, but then it was hard to turn and see her mom.

"It's okay," Meredith said. "Here, just put the quilt over you. You don't have to get in all the way."

Swiveling, Maggie tucked her feet under the quilt and leaned her back on the pillows. She felt her mother's heat warming her, the heat that stuck to whatever she touched. Sometimes that bothered Maggie, the way her mother seemed to be everywhere, in all the rooms she ever entered, and imbedded in Maggie's brain. She wanted her mother to leave her alone. But not now, when it was dark and cold and she felt haunted.

"Something bugging you?" asked Meredith. She reached up and touched Maggie's brown hair and tucked a strand behind her ear.

"I saw 'Schindler's List.'"

"Oh, gosh, Honey, I forgot. I got a note about that. It's pretty upsetting."

"The Nazis say we're Jewish. Are we Jewish?" asked Maggie.

"I suppose we are," said Meredith. "I know we are a combination of things, and that we didn't teach you very well. But sometimes even a small part just dominates, I don't know. Maybe because I'm your mother, and my mother is Jewish too. Maybe there are just some basic attitudes that you get from all the time you spend with your mom. I don't think it's a question of genes. It's something in your heart. It's a basic feeling about life, about taking it as it comes."

"But why would someone want to kill us? They killed just normal people. If Grandma had been there, she would be dead, and we would never have been born."

"You are smart to think of it that way," said Meredith. "But you can scare yourself, too. Sometimes people are evil. I don't like that word, but I don't know what else to call it. Most people, they do something bad, but they still deserve understanding. Even if they kill someone, even if their reasoning is twisted and selfish, we still want to understand them, and that is a good thing. But that sort of killing machine – it's just too much."

"Like the devil was in charge?" asked Maggie.

"Well, I don't think of it as an actual devil – that makes it sound like the people who killed, who turned in their neighbors, who turned their backs, like they weren't responsible – but they were, completely responsible. Maybe calling it evil is just an excuse for not buckling down and figuring out all the social and psychological reasons – I'm sure there are explanations, practical ones. But all those children. It's unbearable. How can people do something so terrible? But some people did." Meredith put her arm around Maggie.

"What about God?" asked Maggie. "Doesn't this just prove that there isn't one?"

"That is a great question, and it puzzles a lot of people who believe in a good God who is in charge of everything. Some of them might say that the Holocaust was part of God's plan, and the plan is ultimately good. I can't accept that. Some think people have free will, that the people do the bad things, and God isn't responsible. Then God isn't so powerful – but that works better for me. And I think there is some randomness too. Sometimes things just happen, and you have to accept that." Meredith paused. "But you are safe. You have a good life, and you live in a good country. I am sorry you have to learn about bad things in the world, but your teachers are right to tell you. Unfortunately, it is probably time."

Maggie rested her head on her mother's shoulder. She closed her eyes, and Meredith stroked her hair. After a few minutes, Meredith shifted her daughter's head onto the pillows and moved herself over to Alex's side of the bed. Under the halo of lamplight, she watched her daughter sleep.

Chapter Fourteen

March 1998

Thursday

Susie stepped from Ron's black Mercedes into a world of valet parking, four star dinners, and waiters who knew his name. Yes, it was snowing when the calendar almost said spring, but who cared when you could glide through the storm on heated leather seats and spend only an instant in the deep freeze before popping under a heat lamp and through a revolving door into the Four Seasons Hotel. Flicking a few snowflakes from her hair, Susie turned to look for Ron, ever the gallant gentleman doing whatever one does with a valet. But she spotted only the two flies in the ointment, her daughter Mindy and Ron's daughter Lauren. The two girls wobbled into each other on high heeled sandals like lost, grouchy egrets.

"All set," said Ron, stepping into the lobby and holding the elevator door for the ladies.

Ron was so handsome, long and lean in his dark suit and cashmere overcoat. Susie hoped she looked all right. She had bought a new dress, dark green with a black belt and a short skirt. The neckline set off the necklace Ron had given her for Valentine's Day, a circle of small diamonds in scalloped platinum. Expensive but not flashy, Susie had thought, admiring it on her collar bone, where it twinkled appropriately. She wondered what sort of necklaces Ron had given Marcia – probably perfunctory pendants selected by his secretary on the occasion of her birthday. The few times Susie had seen Marcia over the years, she was stiff and perfectionist, not the sort to inspire ardor. Ron had seemed that way too, at first, but she had been right about him. He knew how to generate heat. Susie shivered when she thought about their nights together.

They walked across the upstairs lobby next to each other, but not touching. Once her pinkie brushed his hand, but he pulled back and continued across the glossy marble, past an elaborate orchid arrangement and the bridal staircase to the ballroom, and onto the plush carpet. Expensive couches and chairs in inviting arrangements lined the side walls under formally lit abstract paintings flanked by sculptures of crescents and tubes. At the hostess stand, a beautiful young woman in understated ecru gestured that they should follow her to a table for four near the window. Outside, the snow fell in thick angled sheets, giant flakes lit by the city. Inside, all was warm and hushed, a cocoon made out of money.

"I hope we don't get snowed in – though I can think of worse places to be stuck," Susie smiled.

"Yeah, how would that work?" Mindy asked, looking at Susie and Ron. She rested her back, tightly swaddled in an old Turnabout dress, uncomfortably against a curly French chair.

Ron studied the wine list, more like the wine encyclopedia, many pages in a cordovan leather cover.

Gesturing with his index finger, he summoned the sommelier and ordered a bottle of champagne.

"What do we have to celebrate?" asked Lauren glumly. She looked like her mother, a sleek Persian kitten. Her necklace was fancy for a college student – could it be real emeralds? – and Susie wondered for a moment if it had been Marcia's. But no, it was probably costume jewelry from a department store. Susie touched her own necklace self-consciously.

"We're so happy to have you home for spring break," said Ron smoothly. As he chatted with the girls, Susie glanced around the room at the other tables. Most of the women looked regal in tailored suits and perfect shoes. One trashy novice wore an old bridesmaid's dress – she was clearly trying too hard and out of place. Having been to a few of these restaurants now, Susie was starting to understand what to wear, but she still did not feel confident. Maybe soon she would hire a personal shopper to pull her together. She wanted Ron to be proud of her. She also hoped that in a few months she could stop wearing the thong and push-up bra combos she had bought at great expense from Enchante. They had been worth it. But once the deal was sealed, she hoped she could relax, at least a little bit.

The sommelier displayed a champagne bottle to Ron and pulled the cork with a muffled, proper thunk. After Ron sipped his half glass and nodded, the waiter poured the bubbling confection into everyone's glass. The girls were under age, but apparently asking them to fumble through their purses and pull out their driver's licenses was not chic. Lauren stared at her glass resignedly, but Mindy looked pleased.

"To spring break!" said Mindy, and she took a gulp. "Yum!" she pronounced. "This is a lot better than the battery acid they serve at frat parties."

Susie frowned, but Ron simply said, "I'm glad," so that was okay. She would have to speak to Mindy in the Ladies Room after the amuse-bouches. Another waiter came by with silver tongs and a tray with a variety of perfect little rolls and breads. Lauren and Susie selected tiny brioches and shook their heads when the iced butter balls came around, but Mindy and Ron chose larger slices of a plain baguette and helped themselves to several grooved curls.

Now Ron raised his glass. "First, I want to say how happy I am that we are all here together. Susie, you look lovely. And Lauren and Mindy, you two have accomplished so much – you are almost done with your freshman year. That is a great achievement, and we are very proud of you. So, here's to successful new beginnings." They all took a sip of champagne, except for Lauren. Her cat eyes were slits, studying her father.

"You're looking awfully frisky, Dad," said Lauren. "For a man with a dead wife."

"What about my mom?" asked Mindy, polishing off her glass. "Her husband hasn't even been dead six months."

"He has too – six and a half!" interjected Susie.

"And look how great she looks!" finished Mindy. "I know it hasn't been easy, Mom, because it hasn't been easy for me. But my counselor at school says that it will get better with time. She says that in a couple of years...."

"Well," said Ron. "Speaking of new beginnings...."

"All right, enough of this crap, Dad," said Lauren. "What the hell is going on here?"

"The point is, a miracle has happened," said Ron. "We are going to be a family. You two are best friends, and now you will be sisters. I have asked Mrs. Steinmetz to be my wife, and she has accepted."

"God works in mysterious ways, His wonders to perform," said Susie. "Two sad widows, two best friends – isn't it amazing?"

Lauren hurled her glass at her father. It splashed his ear and rolled unbroken under the ice bucket. Mindy just stared at Susie. "Is this a joke?" she asked. "Where's the ring?"

Gritting his teeth, Ron mopped himself off. Susie pulled a box out of her evening bag. "It's here!" She popped the box open and admired the three carat marquise cut ruby all over again. Ron reached over and slid it on her finger. "We wanted it to be a surprise."

Lauren stood, turned, and rushed from the table. Mindy got up and followed her. "Well, I guess they were surprised," said Susie. "Maybe that wasn't such a good idea."

"They'll get used to it," said Ron. "I apologize for Lauren. You do look beautiful. Maybe we should pray for more snow."

"Oh, you are so bad." Susie smacked his thigh and shifted around her thong. "Do you think I should go after them? Maybe they went to the powder room."

"Let's just give them a few minutes. They'll be back." He opened the menu. "Chateaubriand for two?"

"Sounds delicious," said Susie. "Why don't you order for us? You always know the right thing to do."

164

She settled back in her chair with her elbows slightly behind her, to better display her foam-enhanced chest. She knew this was a shock for Mindy, with her father so recently deceased. But there was no sense in everyone mooning around feeling grief-stricken. People needed to pull themselves together and move on. Mindy had a fresh start, with college, new friends, the state of Indiana. Susie wasn't even leaving Glencoe. She had the right to make a few positive changes, to move forward in her life. Mindy was a sensible girl, she would get it, she would come around. Susie wasn't as sure about Lauren. Stepdaughters notoriously despised their mothers' replacements. And Lauren did seem a little tricky, maybe a bit unstable. She was bound to blame Susie, to see her as the culprit in all this. Susie would have to be careful with Lauren.

Friday

"So, they're engaged," said Meredith. She picked up a pencil and put it down again. "Anything else?"

Once again, Lauren Block sat in the chair next to Meredith's desk. Last May, she had arrived distraught, her mother dead in a bloody, one-in-a-zillion accident. Lauren was looking for someone to blame – a propensity with which Meredith, in her line of work, completely concurred. And because he was the only other person in the room, and because he and her mother sometimes fought, Lauren blamed her father. It occurred to Meredith that Lauren also may have fought with her mother. She was a teenage girl, on the brink of leaving the nest for college. Inevitably, there would be friction. Perhaps Lauren blamed her father to deflect guilt from herself. Not that Lauren had murdered her mother, but that she hadn't been kinder when she had the chance. Everyone felt guilty when a loved one died, even under the best of circumstances.

But it was almost a year since her mother died, and Lauren was back. If anything, she looked worse than before, like an unnourishing drink drawn through a straw. Her wrists were thin and knobby, and her jeans hung slack around her thighs. Marcia would have gotten her help, but Lauren had no mother. Meredith wondered if Ron had even noticed.

"Well, it's awful. My mother has been gone for less than a year, and now – Mr. Steinmetz died six months ago, and they're engaged. Everyone else thinks it's part of God's plan, this wonderful miracle, but that makes me sick. How could it be part of God's plan to kill my mother? And Mr. Steinmetz was a nice man, he didn't deserve to die. And what about Mindy – and what about me?"

"The engagement does seem fast, I agree with you," said Meredith. "But of course, that's not enough. Tell me more about Mr. Steinmetz. How did he die?"

"That's the thing," said Lauren. She leaned forward, and her cheeks turned bright pink. Meredith grabbed a tissue and handed it to her. "I know maybe this sounds crazy, but I can't get it out of my head. What if my dad killed him so that he could marry Mrs. Steinmetz?"

"I never heard anything about a police investigation of Mr. Steinmetz's death," said Meredith.

166

"I think I would have heard about a homicide in Glencoe."

Lauren's eyes widened and glittered. "My father is a big deal lawyer, he's very smart, very clever. Mr. Steinmetz was sick, he had cancer, and my dad helped him. My dad never helped anybody. It was weird."

Meredith sat back. She looked at the huge stack of folders on her desk and then glanced at the clock. It was a quarter to two. In fifteen minutes she had to be in court, and it would sure be nice if she could flip through her files before she showed up. "He had cancer," she said.

"Yes. And he died when Mrs. Steinmetz was out of town visiting her daughter, but my dad was around. I mean, what if he planned the whole thing, and he killed my mother and Mr. Steinmetz so that he could marry Mrs. Steinmetz?"

Meredith gazed at Lauren sympathetically. Lauren was only five years older than Maggie, and she hadn't had a mother for a year. And instead of focusing on his daughter, her father was getting married again. Meredith reached out and put her hand on Lauren's arm. She felt the softness of her sweater over two sticks. She looked at the clock again.

"Sweetheart, I'll look into it," she said.

"You will?" said Lauren. Now she looked frightened.

"I don't think there's anything in it, but I will, just to make sure. Don't worry, I won't tell anyone that you came to me. When do you go back to Skidmore?"

"On Sunday."

"Okay. I don't know if I'll be able to get to it before then, but I promise that I will look into it as soon

167

as I can." She picked up a folder. "Do you feel like you are in danger?"

"I'm fine, I'm staying with Mindy. Dad actually likes it. He thinks I'm bonding with my new mother. At least he doesn't sleep over when I'm there." She shuddered. "I'm okay as long as I avoid the bathroom where Mr. Steinmetz died and the garage full of rat poison. That place gives me the creeps."

It was one fifty-five. "Rat poison?" Meredith said. She set the folder back on her desk.

After two hours of proving up speeding cases and recommending traffic school, Meredith began to investigate Lauren's concerns. According to Glencoe Public Safety, Susie Steinmetz called 911 on Sunday, September 21 at about 4:00 p.m. to report that her husband Joel had collapsed in the upstairs bathroom of their home. When the paramedics arrived, they found him dead. Because he had died alone, Public Safety notified the Cook County Coroner's Office. Their call to his oncologist, Dr. Angelo Gold, confirmed that he was treating Joel Steinmetz for colon cancer, and that Joel was on chemotherapy. Dr. Gold signed the death certificate, listing the cause of death as colon cancer, with chemotherapy as a contributing factor. The Coroner's Office then certified the cause of death as colon cancer and released the body to the funeral home for cremation

Last May, Meredith had dismissed Lauren's concerns about her father as a reaction to her own grief and guilt about her mother's death. But to report him twice? To believe him capable of two murders? Meredith decided to talk with Dr. Gold herself.

She parked at the Kellogg Cancer Center, rode the elevator to the second floor, and wound down a long, empty hallway to a reception desk. "I would like to speak with Dr. Gold, please. My name is Meredith Bennett. I'm from the state's attorney's office, and I need to discuss a death certificate that he signed."

"You need an appointment." The receptionist glanced up from a magazine and gestured helplessly toward the deserted waiting room.

"Is he here?" said Meredith. "I really need to talk with him now." She leaned forward. "It's about a suspicious death, kind of a lover's triangle thing. I don't want anyone else to get hurt."

"Oh, wow, why didn't you say so?" Like the gatekeeper to the Land of Oz, the receptionist hurried to open the door to the examining room area and poked her head through a doorway. "Dr. Gold, someone to see you on a matter of life and death."

Meredith walked into the office and nodded. "Meredith Bennett, state's attorney's office. I don't suppose that life-and-death teaser excites an oncologist very much."

Dr. Gold stood and stuck out his hand. Trying not to imagine the ill-people body parts he had touched earlier today, Meredith hesitated, and then grasped it. He was short and grizzled, with the mottled face of an aging beagle, and a humorless, unflappable expression, as if he had seen it all and accepted it. "What can I do for you?" he asked. He neither sat nor offered her a chair.

"In September, you signed a death certificate for Joel Steinmetz. You listed colon cancer as the cause of death, with chemotherapy contributing. Do you remember? He was found dead in his bathroom in Glencoe, and I think the Coroner's Office talked with you."

"Yes, I do remember that. Most of my patients die in the hospital or under the supervision of hospice."

"But Mr. Steinmetz was in neither situation. So, his death was a surprise -- you didn't expect him to die any time soon?"

"Without getting into private medical details, I will say that I was somewhat surprised that he died. But we can't predict the time of anyone's death with certainty." Dr. Gold raised his chin. "The Glencoe Police led me to believe that they had found nothing suspicious."

"Yes, they told me the same thing. Without going into private medical details -- hypothetically, could chemotherapy kill a cancer patient?"

"Chemotherapy is a serious intervention. I never prescribe it unless I believe that the patient needs it to fight his cancer. It's a risk-benefit analysis -- something can always happen with the cancer or with the chemo. I monitor my patients for reactions to the drugs. It's an ongoing analysis. I am very careful. That said, the outcome is not always positive. I do my best, but sometimes these matters of life and death, as you call them, are out of my hands. Anything else?" He frowned.

"Dr. Gold, I'm sorry, don't misunderstand me. I am not questioning your work as a doctor, not at all. But, to be blunt -- if a cancer patient dies unexpectedly in a pool of vomit, might that patient have been deliberately poisoned in some other way by someone else, someone who is not a medical professional?" Meredith blushed. It did sound kind of ridiculous.

Dr. Gold sat down. "Well, that's interesting." He relaxed a little. "You mean, like a poison that someone injected, or put in his food or drink? And the chemo symptoms would mask it?"

"Yes," said Meredith. "That's exactly what I mean."

"Well, I never would have thought of that," said Dr. Gold. "It seems like a one in a million case. And in Glencoe?" He frowned. "I've met Mrs. Steinmetz. She seems – devoted. Normal."

"I know this is a long shot – would you have any recent blood or tissue samples from Mr. Steinmetz?"

"No." He shook his head. "The hospital might have saved some of his tumor, but that surgery would predate the chemo. Blood and such are incinerated. You're serious about this?" Dr. Gold asked.

"I think it's worth doing a little digging. Just in case."

"Was he cremated?"

"Unfortunately, yes."

"Well, it was nice meeting you." Dr. Gold stood again and put out his hand. "I'd better get back to work."

"Thanks very much," said Meredith. She waved as she walked out the door, then headed straight to the restroom to wash her hands.

Chapter Fifteen

Friday Night

Susie Steinmetz's house, a modest white colonial, glowed eerily in the light from an old-fashioned street lamp. Meredith parked on the street and walked up the driveway, where a black Mercedes huddled like a big cat. The last winter's ice clung to the wooden stairs, and Meredith gripped the metal railing to protect herself in case she slipped. She rang the doorbell and stepped back. The front porch was empty, no outdoor furniture, no swing or pots for summer flowers.   After a few moments, the front door opened, and Susie Steinmetz appeared.

Susie's large ruby engagement ring glinted in the artificial light. Ron must have thought that the red stone would complement her hair. Instead, the colors fought, her hair rust, the ring a gleaming drop of blood on her small, white hand. She wore dark pants and a fuzzy green sweater, like a small fur tree, her pale face and bright halo the Christmas angel on top.

"Mrs. Steinmetz? My name is Meredith Bennett. I hope I'm not interrupting your dinner."

Meredith could hear voices coming from the back of the house. Lauren and Mindy must be here, and, judging from the car in the driveway, Ron was too. It seemed a little early for a high-powered bankruptcy lawyer to be back in Glencoe for the evening, but maybe the rules were different for recent widower/fiances. "What can I do for you?" asked Susie, her hand on the door. "This really isn't a good time," she added.

"I'm a prosecutor from the state's attorney's office." Susie's eyes widened. "I have a few questions about your husband Joel's death."

Susie stepped onto the porch and closed the front door. "What are you talking about? Joel died of cancer."

"Yes," said Meredith, "I know that is the official cause of death. Did his death strike you as unusual, given what you understood about the state of his health?"

"No, not at all," said Susie. "I mean, his prognosis was good at the beginning, but he was very sick from the chemo. I shouldn't have left him alone, but I was only gone for a day. Joel insisted that I go, to see our daughter."

"Well, about that," said Meredith. "I'm sure you wouldn't have left him alone if he were too sick to manage, at least not without someone to help him, maybe a friend to check up on him."

"No, of course not," said Susie.

"So, someone looked in on him while you were gone?"

"I don't know for sure. He had a friend who said he would come by, but I don't think he made it. I borrowed his cell phone, and I could get back quickly if Joel needed me, that was the plan. Joel insisted that I go, it was Family Weekend at Indiana, my daughter is a freshman there."

"So, when you returned the friend's phone, did you ask him if he had seen your husband before he died? Who is this friend, by the way?"

Susie flushed. "His name is Ron Block. Our daughters are best friends, and we all became good friends after his wife died."

"Oh, yes," said Meredith. "His wife died in strange circumstances, didn't she?"

"I suppose," said Susie. "Look, I really have to get dinner going." She reached back and pushed the door open. "We both lost our spouses tragically, and we are trying to recover. Please leave us in peace. Good night. Don't come back."

Susie went into the house and closed the door. Meredith could hear the bolt turn. It was time for her to go home to her own children and dinner. She thought she would let the Steinmetz-Block clan simmer for a while.

In Chicago, the end of March, the official start of spring, meant drippy icicles, dirty slush, and fifty degree days interspersed with snow flurries and frozen puddles. The sense of spring was a tantalizing curse, dangling the promise of warmth and green grass, which would not arrive reliably until June. In winter, Meredith knew it would be cold, and she hunkered down or put on lots of clothes. Now began the long, slow tease, full of reversals, that was almost worse than the deep freeze.

Glancing down her street as she headed toward the alley, Meredith noticed a Mercedes parked across from her house. Ron Block couldn't have hopped in his car and beaten her here – anyway, he didn't know where she lived. She knew one other person who drove that car. She could imagine him walking in and turning on all the lights and turning up the heat to show that he was back. She could imagine dinner simmering in a big pot on the stove, an aroma of heat and spice and love wafting through the house and turning it into a home. He had said he would be back in March, and he was – he had kept his word.

Meredith parked in the garage and picked her way down the path to the house. She could hardly wait to get there, to open the door and see him standing tall and grinning and magnetic. He loved her, and he promised to come home, and here he was. She wanted to rush to him, but she had to be careful, the path was slick and treacherous. Fumbling, she pulled her house key from her purse, threw open the door, and practically fell into the kitchen.

There was nothing on the stove. Meredith set down her purse and briefcase and slipped off her boots. The house was quiet. As she walked toward the front hall to hang up her coat, she glanced into the dining room. The table, which she had imagined set for four, with placemats and glasses of wine and milk and maybe even candles, was empty, except for a box of markers and a couple of sheets of white paper. Maggie and Lucy sat in chairs behind the paper, but they weren't drawing. They just sat there. At the head of the table was Shawna.

"I thought they could color until you came home, but I guess they're too old now," she said.

Her hair was still a blonde ponytail, her blue eyes boldly outlined, her mouth full and peach. But she looked tired and tense, a Barbie that had been played with a little too hard, or that had been left forgotten outside in bad weather. She sagged forward, her full breasts protruding from an uncharacteristic thick oatmeal cardigan. She was alive, but she looked unwell. No one said anything, not even Lucy. Then Maggie stood and hurried toward her.

"Mom, I think you should go upstairs and change. Shawna, you need to leave."

"What's going on?" asked Meredith.

Shawna pushed back her chair and stood up. Her belly was enormous, and not from too many daiquiris. "The Miracle of Life," she announced. "I wanted to tell you myself. Do you have any tuna fish?"

Meredith set her coat on the table. She pulled out a chair and sat down. Her stomach spun dizzily, as if she were the pregnant one. Involuntarily, she closed her eyes and rested her forehead on her fist. She didn't even care anymore. "Check the cupboard," she said.

Shawna went into the kitchen. Maggie and Lucy flanked their mother. Each put an arm around Meredith and rested her head on her mother's shoulder, like a reverse pieta.

"I think she should leave," said Lucy. "And then we should get pizza."

"Mom, what do you need?" asked Maggie. Meredith looked up, into the compassionate eyes of a young adult. She knew the transformation was probably temporary, that there would be many scenes and setbacks on the way to maturity -- but it was coming on, like spring. She reached into herself and sat up straight. "It's okay," she said. "Why don't you two go upstairs. Maggie, order some pizza. I'll talk to Shawna until it gets here."

"Come on, Lucy." Maggie reached out her hand, and Lucy took it. Meredith went into the kitchen, where Shawna was mashing tuna fish with mayonnaise in a soup bowl. She and Alex had received those dishes as a wedding present, so long ago.

"When are you due?" she asked.

"In May," said Shawna, licking the spoon. "I had to come home now. They wouldn't have let me fly much longer. Anyway, I wanted to talk to you."

"Why?" asked Meredith. "I don't know what this has to do with me."

"Well – we're a family," said Shawna. "Maggie and Lucy are going to be sisters." Meredith closed her eyes again.

"So. You and Alex are going to move back to Kenilworth, and we'll go on as before. Except with a baby."

"That's the plan," said Shawna. "I think that makes you a grandma," she said, pulling bread out of the refrigerator.

"No, it doesn't," said Meredith. She felt very tired. "You can eat your sandwich, but after that you have to leave." She paused, remembering all that Alex had said to her, and all that he hadn't said. "Shawna – really. What's going on. Are you okay?" Shawna turned and leaned on the counter. She looked enormous and exhausted. "Come on, let's go sit back down." Meredith cut Shawna's sandwich in triangles and picked up the plate, with a placemat and a napkin. She set it all down on the table.

"May I have a glass of water, please?" she asked, like a little girl. Meredith got them both water and sat down too. Shawna stared at her sandwich. "Thank you," she said. Then she looked up. "Have you been cheating on me with Alex?" Her eyes filled with tears.

Meredith wondered if it were possible for her to cheat on Shawna. But she knew what Shawna meant, of course she did. "I haven't seen Alex, except for a few minutes in the airport, in almost a year," Meredith said.

"But you've been talking to him," said Shawna. "An emotional affair." She sniffed.

"Looks like you've had the real deal," said Meredith.

"Yes," said Shawna, lifting her chin. "We are married. What did you expect?"

Good question. Alex and Shawna were married. Had she really expected him to be celibate while they were giving their marriage a chance? Meredith counted backwards. "So you got pregnant seven or eight months ago – in August?" She tried to remember what was happening with Alex in August, what he was saying in his letters, how romantic he had been, whether he had said that he wanted her back. But honestly, what difference did it make? He had sex with Shawna – but more important, he had known that she was pregnant for months, and he never told her. His wife was pregnant – didn't he think that was a relevant fact, something she would want to know and understand? If he could lie to her about something that important, how could she trust anything he said? "What has Alex been telling you?"

"I don't have to say," said Shawna, picking up her tuna sandwich. "Marital privacy. You ought to know that. It's the law." She took a big bite.

Shawna was right. She had all the cards. She had the marriage and the baby and the sandwich. What if Alex did love Meredith, did it even matter? But maybe, if she and Alex loved each other, that was all that mattered. Maybe she had the tuna fish, and all Shawna had was two slices of cold white bread.

"Time to go," Meredith said, standing up.

"But I'm not done," Shawna said. "The Miracle is still hungry."

"I'll get it a baggie," said Meredith. She didn't know if she had ever seen a miracle, but she knew that Shawna wasn't the Virgin Mary, and that this baby wasn't going to turn water into wine or raise the dead. Alex and Shawna had made it the old-fashioned way. It may have been an accident, but it was the result of purposeful human behavior.

Chapter Sixteen

Monday

Susie never got in trouble. She had been to the Skokie Courthouse only once before, to help Mindy out with a speeding ticket. Expecting a professional atmosphere, she had dressed in a somber suit, with a punchy striped blouse for the judge, and she had insisted that Mindy wear the plain, knee-length skirt and crewneck sweater that Susie bought her for college interviews. The slovenly attire of the other offenders surprised her. Even their lawyers wore cheap suits and skewed neckties, their shabby briefcases spewing sheets of dog-eared yellow paper. A prosecutor in a plain blouse and slacks requested arrest warrants, traffic school, continuances, and reduced fines from a judge who shifted papers from one side of her desk to the other. People got a lot of chances, and even after that, consequences weren't as serious as she had expected.

So, Susie climbed the steps to the state's attorney's office with some confidence. True, she was coming to say that she had concealed information from the police. On the other hand, she had no criminal record of any kind, not even a parking ticket. She was a nice mom from Glencoe, a widow. They wouldn't punish her for a little white lie.

"Mrs. Steinmetz?" Meredith Bennett, in a gray pantsuit that blended into her surroundings, approached down the hall, like a staged shot from the ten o'clock news. She might have been cute if she had done something with herself – lose the glasses, a little gel on the curls, bright lipstick, a kitten heel – though the suit fit her well, and the jacket concealed the soft chub that undoubtedly had formed around her middle. Although Meredith was a lawyer, as the fiancé of a much fancier lawyer, Susie felt her superior status.

"Please follow me."

Meredith led her a few doors down, to a bland cubicle with a beat-up desk and a poster instead of a window. Removing her coat to reveal a plum pantsuit and soft mauve blouse, Susie brushed off her chair with a Kleenex. She settled across from Meredith, who shifted some file folders on her desk and leaned forward.

"What can I do for you?" Meredith asked.

"Well," Susie said, blushing. "We talked the other day about my husband Joel's death. You caught me at a bad time, and I did some thinking afterwards. I know it's silly, but I started to worry that you might have the idea that Ron Block had something to do with Joel's death. Of course he didn't, that is ridiculous."

"Why do you say that?" asked Meredith.

"Well, I know him, of course." Meredith looked at her and waited. "Actually, we're engaged. Also, I have this." Susie opened her purse and fumbled around for a moment. "Here. It's Joel's suicide note."

Susie handed Meredith an envelope. Meredith pulled out a sheet of paper and unfolded it.

Dear Susie,

I hope you know that I love you, and that I am very sorry to leave you. Thank you for a wonderful life. I am tired of being sick, and I hate the drain on you and Mindy. You are both young and should live your lives. I know the way this cancer treatment goes. I could linger for years, always going to doctors, feeling nauseous and tired, not able to enjoy my life and ruining yours. It just doesn't make sense to make you and Mindy miserable so that I can hang on as a sick man for a little longer. So, go and live, find someone new, you have my blessing. And take good care of Mindy, I know you will.

Love,
Joel

P.S. It is my last wish that you conceal my suicide from Mindy. I don't want to upset her further. And please cremate me. Thanks.

Meredith looked up. "So you followed his wishes?"

"Yes," said Susie. "I was afraid to tell anyone about the note, in case Mindy found out. I was trying to be a good wife."

Meredith looked at the paper. "Did he usually type his notes?"

"Well – he tried to do things the right way. Maybe he saw this as a legal document. He would want to be sure we could read it too. His handwriting was shaky, since he was sick."

"What would he have typed it on? There aren't any mistakes. Do you have a computer?"

"Joel needed it for his business, and Mindy used it for school." Susie paused. "Why are you asking me all these questions? I came here today as a concerned citizen, to help you out. My poor husband killed himself, and that's it. You don't need to make me feel worse." She stood up. "I would like my note back." She held out her hand, sparkling with the giant ruby ring.

"I'm sorry, I will need to keep this for a little while," said Meredith calmly. "If it's on the computer, you can make yourself another copy."

"Joel deleted it," said Susie. "He didn't want Mindy to find it, remember?"

"I'll get it back to you when we're done with it. I hope you didn't collect any life insurance. That could be a problem for you, now that we know your husband committed suicide."

Susie glared at Meredith, picked up her coat, and walked out. Joel did have a small amount of life insurance, which helped with Mindy's college expenses. But now that Susie was marrying Ron, that was a drop in the bucket. Would Meredith notify the insurance company? Susie doubted it, the woman was just trying

183

to scare her. Heels clicking, Susie scampered down the stairs. That Meredith Bennett, what a witch. Let her try being a single mom and doing the right thing. It wasn't easy, that's for sure.

Well, that was weird, Meredith thought. People went to enormous lengths to protect their loved ones, but she had to hand it to Susie – bringing in a fake suicide note to try to clear Ron was gutsy. She must really love him – or she really wanted to marry him and ride off into the sunset in a shiny Mercedes. But would she want to marry him if she thought he killed her husband? Well, maybe, if she thought he did it for love of her.

And what about Marcia's death via glass table? If Susie were suspicious, surely she would not want to be Wife #2. But women did marry men whose previous wives had died under strange circumstances. Heck, they even married men on death row. And people always thought they were the special ones, or that the guy had changed. Too bad for lousy Wife #1, Wife #2 would grab the brass ring. Or the ruby ring, in this case.

Shawna had married Alex after he cheated on Meredith, and now Shawna was surprised that Alex was cheating on her. And what about Meredith herself? Some people never learned. You just dangled love in front of them, and they went after it like a hungry dog for a strip of bacon. For a strip of bacon soaked in poison, a slow-acting poison that caused a lingering death.

Meredith stopped. She pulled out a phone book and opened to the yellow pages, the letter P, Pest Control. She picked up the phone and punched in the number for the first place listed, AA Ants Away Pest Control Company.

"Hello, my name is Meredith Bennett. I'm a prosecutor, and I'm investigating a case, and I have a few general questions about pest control poisons. Is there someone there I could talk to?"

"This is Audrey," said a friendly woman. "Maybe I can help you."

"That was wonderful," Susie sighed, dismounting. Ron lay on his back in a state of ecstatic contentment. Sex with Susie – it even sounded like a porn movie – was thrilling in a way that sex with Marcia hadn't been for a very long time. He and Marcia did fine, the old once-a-week, somewhat fatigued, no big surprises – mechanical, but also comfortable and friendly, and always grinding to a predictable, acceptable completion.

Ron shouldn't be thinking about Marcia with his naked fiancé beside him, but he couldn't help it. For one thing, they were in Marcia's bed. When they moved to Glencoe she wanted a king size bed, for the luxury, she said. The bed was so big, it was almost like sleeping alone. She had gone to some fancy place and bought beautiful sheets and a down comforter and a thin white quilt with pillows in all shapes and sizes. When he came home in the evening after a long day at work, Ron half expected to find a chocolate mint on the bedside table and a card with the room service menu.

But Susie blew his mind. Ron had never had an affair – he believed in marriage, and besides, sex with

185

coworkers was dangerous and messy, not worth the risk to his career. Once a woman had picked him up at a hotel bar when he was on a business trip. That was quick and strange, and he tried to forget it. But Susie was a dynamo. Forty-three years old, she was young enough to be frisky, but old enough not to embarrass him at law firm partner dinners. She was a grown woman, not a mid-life crisis. And everybody just ate up the widow-widower thing. It was delicious, perfect, kismet – that universe, it knew what it was doing when it threw Ron and Susie together. Never mind the wreckage behind them.

He turned to Susie. She was so lovely, pink and white and perfect, with just a faint crease near her eyes to make her touching and real. He traced a line with his finger from her neck to her navel. She shivered and smiled. Reaching up, she stroked his cheek. Her eyes sparkled. It was a miracle. But it was the flush of early love, the beginning. The feeling was transcendently delightful, but Ron knew it wouldn't last. If they were lucky, he and Susie would grow together, strong intertwined vines. Ron wanted a real family with a wife, not just him and Lauren floating out in space. He didn't know Susie that well, everything had happened so fast. But he knew he was better with a wife.

"Ron," she said, sitting up. She pulled the covers up to her waist, just under her breasts. "I need to talk to you about something."

"Flower arrangements?" he asked, smiling.

"No, the opposite." She grabbed his bicep and leaned over him, her eyes on his, her breasts gently brushing his chest. "Let's get married right away. We don't need a fancy wedding. I just want to be married to you. Let's do it tomorrow. Can we do it tomorrow?"

Ron sat up. "Honey, what's the rush?"

"You don't want to marry me," she said. She started to cry.

"Well, of course I do. But I thought we would do it in the summer, when the girls are home again and the weather is nice. We don't need a big wedding, but wouldn't you like them to be there?" Ron wrinkled his forehead. He didn't know what was bothering her. Women could be so difficult.

"It's just – that Meredith Bennett woman, that prosecutor. She came over a few days ago. I can't stand her."

"Yeah, I remember her. She was annoying after Marcia died, she showed up at the shiva, if you can believe it. What did she want?" He paused. "Does she think I had something to do with Marcia's death?"

"I don't think so," said Susie, "she didn't talk about that. She thinks you killed Joel."

Ron stared. "That is crazy," he said. "Joel died of cancer."

"I want to get married now," said Susie. "Once we're a team, nothing can hurt us. She doesn't know anything, she's making it all up. Anyway, I went to see her yesterday. I told her that Joel killed himself. I showed her the suicide note."

"Susie, what are you talking about? Did Joel kill himself?"

"No, of course not. I wrote the note. But I didn't want her snooping around you."

"But Susie – you should have talked to me. Who knows what she thinks now?"

"She thinks Joel killed himself, that's all. She's not that clever. If she were, she would have a better job. I was trying to protect you!" Susie started to cry again.

"Protect me from what? I didn't kill Joel, he died of cancer!" Ron looked at her, confused.

"All right, never mind, I made a mistake. I just want to put everything behind us, start fresh. I was trying to help."

"I still don't get it. Why do you think I need your help? Do you think I killed Joel while you were in Indiana? I was busy with work, I didn't even visit him. I know I should have, I feel terrible about it – but that's not a crime." Ron sat back, horrified. "Do you blame me?"

"Of course I don't. I – blame myself. I never should have left him alone."

"Susie, My Dear – I think you are letting your feelings of guilt make you do crazy things. You didn't kill Joel. Neither of us did. He was sick, and he died, that's all. We both did our best, but we couldn't save him." Ron put his arms around her.

"I couldn't save Joel, and you couldn't save Marcia," Susie said. "Just the same."

"Just the same," said Ron. He pulled back, but he held Susie's shoulders and looked at her. "We're going to have to talk to Meredith Bennett, tell her the truth. I'll go with you."

"No. We can't. It will only make things worse. We have to leave it alone. How can you be so calm?"

"Because I know we didn't do anything wrong. And because I know we are meant to live happily ever after together."

"How can you say that? There are injustices, and that woman is a snoop. Why do I have to tell you that, you're the lawyer. And you're a man of action. You make things happen. That's one of the things I love about you." Susie leaned over and kissed Ron hard. Her lips were firm and insistent. "We'll get married tomorrow," she whispered. "Then we can keep each other's secrets." But her hand had started to explore, and he wasn't really listening.

Chapter Seventeen

Tuesday

Meredith stood under the portico at 213 Maple Hill Road. When she lifted her face to breathe the warming air, an icicle dagger detached from a second floor gutter and crashed to the ground inches from her feet. Accidents happen, she thought. And sometimes, they don't. She rang the doorbell.

Ron Block answered. At eight a.m. he was still home, but dressed precisely in a pin striped suit, a starched white shirt, and a peacock tie. He looked clean and rich and ready for another lucrative day of helping corporations avoid paying their bills.

"Sorry to bother you so early. Meredith Bennett, state's attorney's office," she said.

"I know who you are. We were planning to call you anyway. Please, come in." Ron ushered Meredith into the marble hallway. "Would you like a cup of coffee?"

Surprised, Meredith followed Ron to the back of the house, the once forbidden kitchen. Dressed in a cashmere sweater and camel skirt, Susie Steinmetz perched at the new kitchen table next to a nibbled sesame bagel and a large mug of coffee. Here they all were, in the very spot where Marcia Block had bled to death eleven months ago. As she lay on the floor pumping out her life, did Marcia have any inkling that in less than a year a new almost-Mrs.-Block would be munching breakfast in her beautiful home? Susie stood up.

"No coffee for me, thanks," Meredith said. "Please, both of you, have a seat."

"I hope this won't take long," Susie said. "We're going downtown."

Ron pulled out a chair next to a glass of orange juice and a bowl of bran flakes. "Well, let's start with you," said Meredith, turning to him. "Why were you going to call me?"

"Susie has something to tell you."

"You do?" said Meredith.

"No, I don't," said Susie, staring at her plate.

"Well," said Ron. "I guess she doesn't. What brings you here?"

"I wanted to talk to you about your wife's death."

"What about it?"

"So, it must have happened right here – right about where Susie is sitting?"

Susie rolled her eyes and turned white. "Go on," said Ron.

"I understand congratulations are in order."

"Who told you that?" asked Ron.

"Actually, Lauren," said Meredith. "And then Susie. But it must be public knowledge, the ring and all."

"You talked to Lauren?" He frowned. "Leave my daughter alone."

191

"She came to me. Twice, in fact. So, I looked back at the statements you gave to the Glencoe police. Lauren was downstairs in the kitchen before your wife fell, correct?"

Ron looked confused. "No, certainly not. She was up in her room asleep."

"But you were talking on the phone, roaming around the first floor. You were working, you were distracted, that's what you said. Isn't it possible that Lauren was with Marcia when she fell – that she and her mother were having an argument – mothers and teenage daughters fight, that's a fact -- and that Lauren gave her mother a push? I mean, obviously she didn't mean to kill her, but maybe she pushed her, and you have been trying to protect Lauren, and Lauren has been trying to protect herself?"

Susie looked surprised but started to nod. "It does make a sort of sense."

Ron stared at Susie. "What are you doing? You're willing to throw my daughter under the bus? That's ridiculous. It was an accident!"

"Lauren seems perfectly willing to implicate you. She says you and Marcia were fighting all the time, and that Marcia thought you were seeing other women."

"That little bitch," said Susie. "She's just jealous, that's all."

"Jealous of what?" asked Meredith.

"Of me – that Ron and I found each other – that we're finally happy. I'm sorry, Ron, but you can't protect Lauren forever. She's an adult, she has to take responsibility for her actions." Ron stared at her and shook his head.

"You can't prove anything," said Ron. "Because it was an accident."

"You're probably right," said Meredith. "About the proof at least. Which brings me to you, Susie."

"I definitely wasn't there," said Susie, holding up her hands.

"Were you responsible for making your husband's meals?" Meredith asked.

"Whoa, way to switch it up. Why do you ask?"

"I think we should talk about your husband's death. Please answer the question."

"I'm not much of a cook," said Susie. "Anyone can tell you that. Anyway, Joel killed himself."

"Now, we all know that's not true," said Meredith. "Nobody types a suicide note, and nobody's wife hangs onto it for six months. When we examine your computer, I'm sure we will find that you typed that note last weekend. Which leads me to wonder -- what really happened to your husband? Is what we have here a case of two lucky widows finding each other – or of two murderers who killed their spouses and will, at best, be looking over their shoulders for the rest of their lives?"

"If anyone killed Marcia, it was Lauren," said Susie. "You said so yourself. Anyway, I'm not worried. We're getting married today."

"Meredith, it's time for you to leave," said Ron. "If you have any more questions, you'll have to talk to our lawyers."

Standing in the hall, Meredith opened the front door and then slammed it. She was still inside. She heard Ron's voice.

"Joel shouldn't have died. He had a good prognosis. But he was so sick. All that poison in your garage – poison for rodents. I thought I was helping you both, I thought it was a mitzvah. Susie, what did you do?" He sounded like he was going to cry.

"But what about Marcia?" whimpered Susie. "Why is it okay for you? Joel was going to die sooner or later. If I did anything, it was just a little push."

"The wedding is off," Ron said. "Joel was a good man, and Lauren is my daughter. I have to think. I want you out of here."

"But I need you. Mindy needs you. Please."

"Get out," said Ron.

Meredith hoped that Susie's sobs muffled the sound of the door as she sneaked outside. Susie was right to want to get married. If she and Ron were a team, a real family, Meredith could not penetrate their defenses. But a father bear protects his cub from outsiders, no matter what.

Meredith had known from the beginning that she would never be able to prove anything about Marcia Block's death. Even if someone shoved her in a moment of anger, her death was certainly unintended. And she may well have simply lost her footing. But Joel Steinmetz's death – that was something else. The minute she arrived at work, Meredith would go to court to obtain a search warrant for the Steinmetz house. With any luck, Glencoe Public Safety would find a computer hard drive with a suicide note written over the weekend, a partially used box of rodenticide in the garage, matching arsenic traces in the refrigerator, and a decorative urn of cremated remains laced with the same poison. Susie had committed an evil act, the deliberate, premeditated murder of her husband for her own personal gain. Meredith would not let her get away with it.

Maggie took her key off the clip attached to her backpack, unlocked the front door, tripped over the mail, and hung her coat on one of the hooks her mother had pounded into the wall because Maggie and Lucy would never go through all the steps needed to use a hanger. What was the point, she was just going to have to take the coat down again tomorrow. Being an adult was a parade of repetitive time-wasters – fold your clothes, make your bed, put away the crackers. And she had to go to school so early – the bus came at 7:10 a.m. – why would she sacrifice precious minutes of sleep to pull up some blankets she was going to pull back down in fifteen hours? So what, it would look better? Who saw her room? If her mother didn't stick a Pop-Tart in her hand when she was staggering out the door, Maggie wouldn't even eat breakfast.

Lucy would be home from middle school in 45 minutes. Some lunatic sadist had decided that the junior high kids should go to school the earliest, it made no sense. But Maggie did enjoy this afternoon time to herself. She always did her homework first thing, before Lucy started annoying her – get your responsibilities out of the way, and then you can relax.

And she had the first lunch period, at like 10:30 a.m., so she was always starving when she got home. She liked to make a really good snack and enjoy it in the dining room with her school books spread out -- *Seventeen* recommended a healthy, high energy treat with protein to keep her full until dinner. She rinsed a green apple, cut it in slices, and arranged them in a saucer. Then she scooped out a big spoon of peanut butter and set it in the hole in the middle. She poured a mug of milk, added a packet of instant cocoa mix, and nuked it in the microwave. The Spice Girls probably sat down to the same snack after a hard day of singing and dancing. Wiggling to her mental soundtrack while waiting for the cocoa, Maggie checked the magnetic white board stuck to the refrigerator. "Please put the chicken in the oven at 350 at 4:30." Underneath that her mother had hung a piece of paper headed "COUNTDOWN FOR NEW TRIER CLASS OF 2002."

All that capitalization made Maggie nervous. Didn't they understand how much pressure they were putting on kids? She had suffered through the High School Placement Test at 8:30 on a Saturday morning in December, could they make it any worse. Her mother had dragged her to the Academic Life Information Night in January and to the All About Electives Information Night two weeks later. To top it off, at the end of January her totally embarrassing test results arrived. Maggie had scored in the 89th percentile nationally, which was the 46th percentile at New Trier. Basically, she flunked it. Her mother said it was all a bunch of baloney, Maggie was a hard worker, which would get her far in this world. Now it was March, she had met the Course Selection Deadline, signing up for all the normal classes a boring, average kid has to take if she wants to graduate. The Physical Exam Required for First Day Attendance was not her problem. No sense in staring at this creep show ever again. Maggie pulled the COUNTDOWN out from under the air-plant-in-a-shell magnet they had bought at the Orlando Airport because her mother thought it was funny and shoved it in the junk drawer.

Okay, she had everything arranged perfectly. A flowered plastic placemat was on the dining room table, on the long side facing the kitchen, so that no one breaking into the house could sneak up on her. Cocoa steaming enticingly in the upper right corner, Maggie held a dipped apple slice in her left hand and a pencil in her right. Chewing, she attempted to graph the equation $x^2 + 2x - 3 = 0$ on the lined paper in the center of the placemat. The doorbell rang. Drat that Lucy, she was too lazy to use her key. Maggie hauled herself up, marched into the foyer, and threw open the front door. Yup, it was Lucy all right. But behind her stood their father, holding a humungous bouquet of red roses and a velvet heart-shaped box of candy that he must have bought on sale as a joke.

"Maggie!" he said, throwing open his arms and grabbing her in a hug. "I've missed you!"

Maggie pulled back. "I'm surprised to see you, Dad. I have to do my homework." Silently, Lucy grabbed the candy box from her father and streaked into the kitchen.

He frowned for a moment and then bounced back. "Well, that's good that you're doing your homework. Maybe I can help you."

"I'm fine," she said. But she wasn't fine. What was he doing here? Everything was all arranged, they were on it. They had checked all the squares on the COUNTDOWN list. Dinner was in the fridge, ready to go. If she did her homework now, she could watch "Buffy the Vampire Slayer" tonight. She was pretending

197

she was not about to have a brand new baby half-brother or half-sister, a situation which was really annoying and embarrassing and made her mother upset. She loved her father, but honestly, life was calmer without him. Because when he and her mom were together, sometimes Maggie was the only adult in the room.

He hung his coat on a hook and set the roses in the kitchen sink. Then he walked into the dining room, and she wished he wouldn't. This was her private space, her time to regroup after a hard day of conjugating Spanish verbs and deciding whether short stories were about man versus man or man versus society. What about teenager versus screwed-up parents? When were they going to read realistic stories like those?

He sat down next to her at the table and took an apple slice. Her cocoa was cold. "So," he said. "Learn anything interesting lately?"

She looked at him suspiciously. "We learned about the Holocaust."

"Bummer," he said. "How was that?"

"He would have killed you too. Hitler, I mean. At least when you were married to Mom. Maybe he wouldn't anymore."

"I still have a Jewish family," he said.

"Maybe you do, and maybe you don't," said Maggie. "I don't know the rules exactly."

"Well, you are my children, and I love you. I claim you."

"You don't claim Mom," said Maggie. "I don't want to talk about this. I need to put the chicken in, and I have to do my math."

"You're right," he said. "Is it okay if I sit in the living room for a while? I'll try not to bug you."

"Fine," she said. She couldn't protect her mother from this. She was just a kid.

Even though Meredith had made a lot of chicken, they all agreed it would be best to have this discussion in a public place, and away from the children. So, Meredith served Maggie and Lucy ample portions of baked chicken, rice, and cooked carrots and left them with strict instructions to load the dishwasher, finish their homework, and collegially watch teenage girls plunge stakes into vampires' hearts until she returned home with dessert. Meredith, Alex, and Shawna sat beneath the soaring bronze pillars of The Cheesecake Factory. It was like a Mayan Temple, if Mayan Temples served fish tacos and cheeseburgers instead of performing human sacrifices. They sat in a booth, Alex and Shawna facing Meredith like co-defendants before a judge who was trying her damnedest not to run screaming from the courtroom. To placate the waiter, who had introduced himself as Boris and who was clearly fed up with refilling their ice water and waiting for them to read their menus, they had all ordered dessert, Boris's choice, and decaf, a nod to Shawna's unborn child. With a flourish, Boris set a wedge of Snickers cheesecake in front of Meredith, chocolate chip cookie dough cheesecake in front of Alex, and a huge slab of fudge cake with whipped cream in front of Shawna. No one touched a fork.

"It was an accident," said Alex.

"And by that you mean what – you didn't know you were screwing her, you thought it was – me?"

"No chance of that," said Shawna.

"We were trying to get along. I didn't think she would get pregnant."

"And, what is your profession again, Dr. Bennett?" asked Meredith.

"You couldn't expect me to spend a whole year celibate."

"We didn't do it that often," offered Shawna. "I guess this baby just wanted to be born."

"So the baby did it," said Meredith.

"Or God," said Shawna. "Maybe this is a really special baby that will make the world a better place."

Jabbing her fork into the heart of her cheesecake, Meredith resisted the urge to pull it back, flinging Snickers onto the foreheads of the idiots across from her. They deserved the mark of Cain. On the other hand, Shawna and Alex were the ones married to each other. Why did they have to explain themselves to her? "Putting that to one side for the moment – Alex, why didn't you tell me that Shawna was pregnant?"

"I wanted to explain in person."

"Okay. Go for it."

"Well, as I said, it was an accident." The song, "I didn't know the gun was loaded," started playing in Meredith's head. "I know that argument doesn't impress you much, but it's true. It was an impulse – one that I regret."

"You don't want our baby?" Shawna asked. She started to well up.

"How do I know it's my baby?" asked Alex. Shawna visibly recoiled, like she had been shot. Meredith remembered what it felt like to be pregnant and vulnerable. She reached across the table and touched Shawna's hand.

"I still have a lock of your hair," said Meredith, looking at Alex. "We can test it, when the baby is born."

"That's a little ridiculous, don't you think? Okay, the baby is probably mine. It's mine. I'm just upset. This is a minefield. I want to take care of the baby. But I meant what I said."

"You are married to me. We're having a child," said Shawna. "We'll be a family. This will fix everything, Alex. I'll be a great mom, I'll be happy, and you'll love the baby. And you'll love me too. You still love me, I know it. You have to."

Shawna was trembling. Her face was tired, and she put her hand on her belly protectively. She was having a baby, Alex's baby, and she needed him. It was one thing to fight her when she was skinny and saucy, in kick-ass boots and a tiny, tight skirt. But Meredith didn't have the stomach for this.

Alex felt it too. "I will take care of all my children. Men have kids from more than one spouse. It's not that strange."

"But you can only have one wife," said Shawna. "And that's me."

"Shawna is right," said Meredith, wondering if she had heard herself correctly. Well, even a blind squirrel found a nut sometimes, as her grandpappy said.

Alex looked at Meredith. He reached across the table and took her hand. She tried to pull away, but he kept a firm grip. "I made a terrible mistake – more than one. I did it, and I am so sorry, you have no idea. I feel like I am on some funhouse ride, and I can't get off, and the longer I stay on, the worse things become. Meredith,

201

you have to let me off. I love you. I want to come home."

Shawna gasped. She started to struggle, she wanted to run from the table, but she was pinned by her own belly between Alex and the wall. "I hate you both, I want to go!" she cried. "I can't sit here and listen to this, it's cruel!"

"Is everything okay? How are you liking those desserts?" asked Boris, reaching over to pour decaf into their untouched mugs. "Not too hungry tonight, eh? I'll get you some to-go boxes. How many do you need?"

Alex looked at Boris like he was from Mars instead of Skokie. "Three would be fine," said Meredith.

"No problemo," said Boris. "And take your time."

Meredith looked around the room. Across from them, a young couple, a man and a woman, shared a huge platter of nachos with olives on top. Pulling on chips, thin strings of cheese ran between them. A family sat behind them, a harried woman and a man who had come straight from work, in a jacket and tie. Their children, two toddlers, popped up and leered at the nacho couple, while the grandma fed Cheerios to a baby in a highchair. An old couple followed the host to their seats. As the host turned to chat them up, the wife teetered, the husband's hand hovering over her back like a talisman. Life was precious and short. Everyone did the best they could. People were selfish, and they made mistakes, but they tried.

"The most important thing," said Meredith, "is to protect the children. Maggie and Lucy are still kids, but they are growing up, and they are watching us, to see how adults behave. And that little one in there,"

Meredith nodded toward Shawna's stomach, "is their sister or brother."

"Brother," said Shawna.

"Oh!" said Meredith. She blanched – a son for Alex! -- and then composed herself. "However he came to be, he is almost here, and he needs love and protection. Shawna, you always helped me with the girls when I needed it, and I'm sure they would love to help you with their little brother. We are all connected."

"Is this the circle of life?" asked Shawna. "Because I'm going to puke."

"I agree," said Meredith. "About the puke part. We are all connected, but we are not one big happy family. But we can try to get along." She turned to Alex. "You need to sort yourself out. If you can't be loyal to Shawna, you need to leave her."

"I love you," said Alex. "I want to come home."

"I'll take you to the cleaners," said Shawna to Alex.

"That's fine," said Meredith. "Go for it. But we will all help you with the baby. We are going to be in each other's lives, like it or not. Alex," she said, turning to him, "I heard you about the funhouse ride. But I have to know that, once you get off, you won't get on the spinning teacups."

Alex looked confused.

"You need to get a divorce. Give Shawna the house if she wants it, give her plenty of money, and take care of your kid. Buy yourself a condo near Plaza del Lago."

"No Man's Land?" He made a face.

"That's where you belong, don't you think? And after you've done all that, if it's going well, and if I'm still available, you may ask me out. That's all I've got."

Boris brought over three Styrofoam containers and the check. "I don't think I can eat this," said Shawna. "Ever."

"That's okay, I don't think any of us can." Meredith loaded all the cake into one box and shut the lid. "I'll bring these home to Maggie and Lucy."

"I just got back here today," said Alex, turning to each of the women. "Where can I sleep?"

"You're a big boy," said Meredith. "Figure it out. Thanks for the cake." She stood and put her coat on. "By the way, I love you too. Asshole." She left.

Chapter Eighteen

April 1, 1998

Ron sat on a polyurethane chair next to a postage stamp pool on the first floor of the Comfort Inn in Saratoga Springs, New York. Although the calendar said spring and the landscape said winter, the pool area was a constant tropical summer, the air thick and humid, the windows festooned with artificial ferns. When Lauren walked in Ron turned, and a large plastic frond looming over his chair poked him in the eye.

She was wearing a heavy, gray sweater that tied around the middle. It looked familiar – Ron thought that he had given it to Marcia as a gift, maybe for Chanukah, ages ago. He didn't know Lauren had taken it. She had always been thinner than her mother – she was a teenager, after all – but the sweater swallowed her. She stood in front of him, her cat eyes gleaming, her dark hair shiny and perfect.

He stood up. "I'm so glad to see you," he said. "Thank you for meeting me here, I know it's awkward. I want to see the campus later, of course, and your dorm room. We could take your roommate out for dinner. What's her name again?" He put his arms out for a hug.

She stood still, appraising him. He was wearing red swimming trunks and a Chicago Bears tee shirt, and his feet were bare. "You need a new bathing suit, Dad," she said gravely. "I think you've had that one since I was in third grade."

"Probably," he said. "I don't swim much." He paused. "Despite living three blocks from the lake. I guess I was always working."

"I guess," she said. "I do remember going in hotel pools with you sometimes. I don't want to do that now, it's too cold. You said there's a Jacuzzi, right?"

Ron nodded and pointed to the corner behind her. "I'll get it started," he said.

He removed his tee shirt, walked over to the wall, and pushed the red button under the life preserver. The water in the small, round pool began to churn, like a witch's cauldron. He stepped in carefully, adjusting to the heat, feeling its fingers reach up his chest to redden his face. Gradually, he perched on the bench between two spewing jets.

Across the room, Lauren removed her sweater and her blouse. Stepping out of her shoes and pants, she stood for a moment in a blue bikini before finding a towel to wrap herself. She was so thin, every rib delineated, like an abandoned puppy who had been roaming the streets for weeks in search of scraps and a scratch under the chin. But that was ridiculous. He had paid for a Skidmore meal plan. She dropped the towel, clambered into the bubbling stew, and sat across from him, as far away as she could get.

"At least there's no one else here," Ron said. "I thought there might be little kids running around and making a lot of racket."

"Dad, it's nine a.m. No one is awake."

"We've always been early risers. You got up in the morning and came downstairs, even on the weekend."

"I had a lot of homework," said Lauren. "And Mom never let me stay up very late."

"She was trying to take care of you."

"I know," said Lauren. "So, what did you want to talk about? This is a funny place to do it. Kind of nice, though. I've been cold all winter, but this is warming me up. I heard about Mrs. Steinmetz. Mindy told me. I can't believe it. What's going to happen to her?"

"Well, she's in jail for now," said Ron. "I got her a good lawyer, for Mindy's sake. Of course, it's over between us."

"I'm sorry, Dad. I know you really liked her."

"I guess I didn't know her very well. It's just sad, all the way around. Joel might have lived. But I guess she lost faith, I don't know, maybe she just wanted my money. But if she really thought he was going to die, why couldn't she have waited? I'm sorry, I shouldn't be talking to you about this."

"It's okay, I'm not a baby anymore." She inched a little closer to him. "You're a catch, Dad – and not just for the money. You just lost your wife. Maybe she was afraid she needed to act fast, or someone else would grab you."

"Maybe. Okay, this is hard. We need to talk about your mother. We need to clear the air. I think it would help us both. You're not eating enough."

"I'm fine, Dad."

"No, you're not. We are not." He paused. "I'm not angry, I promise – but I know you went to that prosecutor and said you thought I killed your mom."

Lauren looked flustered. "I don't think I said that, exactly. But you told the police I was still upstairs when it happened. I said it too, you're the lawyer, I thought maybe it was better somehow. But it was weird. I didn't know what was going on."

"I was trying to protect you," Ron said. Lauren looked at him skeptically. "Let's go over that morning."

"Okay," said Lauren, "I guess. You go first."

The water roiled around them. Ron took his arms out, to cool off. "So, we were all in the kitchen. Your mother and I were cleaning up from breakfast, and you were standing around, since you don't eat anything. And we were having a discussion. An argument."

"About college. The deadline was coming up for accepting my spot. And Mom didn't like my decision. She insisted that I go to Skidmore, and I didn't want to. I decided I would rather go to Indiana with Mindy. I got into the honors program. I would have been fine."

"Right," said Ron, wrinkling his nose. "We both thought you were making a mistake. And then she saw the spider, and she got out the ladder. And while she was climbing up, that's when she told you."

"She said she had already sent in all the forms accepting Skidmore. She was swishing around at the ceiling, and she seemed pretty agitated. She said she knew she had probably overstepped, but that I was dragging my feet, and she was worried I would miss the deadline. So, she sent in the deposit and signed my name."

"And you started yelling, and the phone started ringing – I was expecting a work call, so I got distracted. And the next thing I knew, your mother was on the ground."

"So, you didn't see what happened?" asked Lauren.

"No," said Ron. "Nothing."

Lauren paused. "Well, I guess I was yelling, but I was so mad. And then -- like you said, she was on the ground."

"So, she just fell off," said Ron. "We both agree. It was an accident. Sometimes, things just happen."

"But why did you lie to the police?"

"It seemed easier. If they knew we were fighting, it would have confused things. And I wanted to protect you. Since you were there."

"You wanted to protect me, and I accused you." Lauren started to cry.

"It's okay, Honey." He moved close to her. "I understand. I don't blame you for anything. Not one thing." He reached out and put his arms around her. She put her arms around his neck and sobbed into his naked chest like a little girl.

The water stopped moving. It was calm and quiet, like a hot bath. "I guess it needs restarting," said Lauren. "I can get out and push the button again." She started to move, but Ron gently took hold of her arm. "Wait," he said. "It's nice like this. Peaceful."

They sat and felt the water cradling them. Ron put his arms back in and closed his eyes. They had been through so much. He felt he could live like this forever, in a hot tub with Lauren, shutting out the world. He had never felt as close to anyone, and simultaneously he had never been as aware that two people, even a parent and a child, can never know each other. But that was okay. She was his daughter. He loved her. He accepted it.

After a few minutes he opened his eyes. Lauren was crouched in the middle, submerged except for her head. But her perfect hair was wet, her face covered with drops. Ron came to the middle with her. He dunked his head, and they looked at each other. He took her hands.

"Tell Mindy we will take care of her. She can live with us this summer. She is like a sister to you. She is part of our family."

"Thanks, Dad."

"One more thing." Ron put his hand on his daughter's head and pushed gently. They both went under water and came up. "Blessed art thou, Lord our God, who has blessed us with life, sustained us, and enabled us to reach this season."

"I've always liked that one," said Lauren.

"Me too," said Ron. They crouched for a moment, dunked again, and stood up. "Let's go get some pancakes. There's a Golden Corral down the street."

"That sounds awesome," said Lauren. "I'm hungry." They stepped out of the water, grabbed their towels and belongings, and headed to Ron's room to change for breakfast.

About the Author

Hope Sheffield grew up in Rochester, New York, and then moved to Memphis, Tennessee, where she graduated from high school. She earned a degree in psychology at Harvard College. Although she greatly enjoyed Harvard Law School, her legal career was brief. She and her husband have four adult daughters and a teenage son. The author now lives with her husband and son on Chicago's North Shore. *The Glass Table* is her fourth Meredith Bennett mystery, following *Blood Mother*, *The Inflatable Man*, and *Turnabout*.

www.ingramcontent.com/pod-product-compliance
Lightning Source LLC
Chambersburg PA
CBHW021033130626
46552CB00005B/1820